FROZEN HEART

Jenna has reached a low point in her life — she's lost her business, her home and her boyfriend. Reluctantly, she goes to live with her stepfamily, where she's treated like Cinderella. Then she meets Gus, a handsome stranger with his own problems. When they fall in love it looks like Jenna will get her own fairytale happy-ever-after — but there are troubles to overcome before Jenna and Gus can finally reach for a life and love together.

CAROL MACLEAN

FROZEN HEART

Complete and Unabridged

LINFORD
Leicester

First published in Great Britain

First Linford Edition
published 2013

A catalogue record for this book is available
from the British Library.

ISBN 978–1–4448–1720–1

Published by
F. A. Thorpe (Publishing)
Anstey, Leicestershire

Set by Words & Graphics Ltd.
Anstey, Leicestershire
Printed and bound in Great Britain by
T. J. International Ltd., Padstow, Cornwall

This book is printed on acid-free paper

1

'I have no choice,' Jenna said, but her hand hovered hesitantly above the telephone. Could she really make the call?

Ann lifted the cherry red phone and placed it firmly out of reach on the counter top, where it loomed large in Jenna's mind like a beacon.

'You must think again,' Ann said. 'Surely there must be an alternative.'

But there wasn't. Jenna gazed around in despair at the empty shop. It was small and had been, until recently, cosy and welcoming with the scents of chocolate and vanilla, mint and other sweet flavours. Now the glass counter, where she'd so proudly displayed the baking, was empty. A 'for sale' sign hung at an angle across the plate glass window. Beyond she could see the wild, grey sea and the fishing boats in the

1

harbour bobbing up and down with its force.

'I made a big mistake coming back up here,' she said with a sigh.

'Don't be silly,' Ann said, moving around briskly, filling the kettle with water. At least the kettle and two mugs were still here. Everything else was packed and sorted. It would be sold or stored or recycled, depending. 'You couldn't have predicted the credit crunch. No-one did. Besides, your bakery shop was a success for five years so let's have no more talk of mistakes. The question is, what are you going to do now?'

Jenna smiled fondly, at her best friend. What would she do without her? She was always a source of help and support and fun too. She kept her spirits high and was able to see the positive side to everything. Which was more than Jenna could do right now. She was twenty six years old and had lost everything. She had no job and, since yesterday, no boyfriend. She had nowhere to live either. The house had to go along with the shop to pay her debts. If she was careful she would have a small amount left over to live on for a while. How she would pay for rent and food in the long term, she had no idea.

When her father died six years ago, he'd left her with a reasonable inheritance. It had brought her much needed freedom from her home circumstances. She'd used the money to return to the Western Highlands of her childhood, to follow her dream. She'd learned the art of baking from her mother at an early age and with that and patisserie training at cookery school, she was able to create her own hand-made cakes and pastries to sell in her tiny shop.

There she'd met Ann, who owned the clothes shop next door. Ann had a constant stream of mums and kids buying cheap but cheerful clothes in her affordable racks and Jenna was always grateful when a few would spill over into her tiny shop afterwards.

They made an odd pair of friends.

Ann was so tall and willowy, with straight platinum hair, beautiful like a model, while Jenna was of average height with brown shoulder-length hair and quite ordinary, or so she thought. She would melt easily into a crowd. She had 'one of those faces' as her stepmother Lisette had been fond of telling her. She wasn't special at all. That had been drummed into her by Lisette and Shelley until she quite believed it. Only with her father had she felt unique and loved. She missed him still so much.

Ann put a mug of hot tea down in front of her. The fragrant steam helped lift her spirits from her miserable thoughts.

'You need a holiday,' Ann told her, with a critical eye. 'You don't look well at all. In fact, you look downright peaky. A week in some winter sunshine abroad is just the tonic you need.'

Ann was right. Jenna knew she wasn't at her best. She'd lost weight with the worry of her business, but instead of looking slim, she was scraggy and her clothes hung unattractively on her. Her hair was lank despite frequent conditioning, its copper gleam quite disappeared. Her skin was pasty and she couldn't shift the cold she'd harboured for the last couple of months.

'There's no way I can afford a holiday just now.' She shook her head. 'I have to be realistic, Ann, about my future. I need a place to stay until I can find a job.'

They both looked at the telephone and back at each other.

'Come and stay at mine,' Ann said.

'It's a kind offer, Ann, but you simply don't have room.'

Ann lived in a tiny one-bedroom flat above her shop. It was cramped even for one.

Jenna blew her nose and pulled more tissues from the hanky box. She carried it around with her as much as her handbag these days. She shivered as a rackety breeze pushed under the shop door and buttoned up her thick, woollen cardigan more tightly. If it didn't look ridiculous, she'd have added a woolly hat and gloves it was so cold. November was such a dreary month, nothing but grey light and darkness to look forward to. She felt her spirits sinking again and made an effort to smile as Ann watched her with concern.

'Sorry Jenna but I have to go. I've left Cammie in charge but you know what she's like. She's a lovely girl but so shy she wouldn't dream of talking to the customers.'

'I'll be fine.' Jenna waved her away. 'I need to tidy up in here anyway. That'll warm me up.'

* * *

She found the act of sorting and dusting therapeutic. There was no need to think about other things. She could make simple decisions such as keep this filing cabinet and throw out that cardboard box. She even whistled while

6

she mopped the floor until a bout of coughing overcame her and she had to stop, leaning over the mop handle until the spasm lessened. She didn't hear the door open behind her until he spoke.

'Jenna?'

She turned happily, letting the mop drop with a clatter to the floor. 'William! You came back.'

He looked uncomfortable, his feet shifting in their scruffy trainers, his big hands shoved in his pockets. She longed to run her fingers through his long hair as though nothing had changed. Perhaps nothing had, she thought hopefully.

'No, no . . . ' he flushed, 'I meant what I said yesterday.'

Jenna's heart sank like a lead, leaving a raw, painful hole in her chest.

'I don't understand,' she whispered, praying the tears wouldn't well up again. 'We were happy together, weren't we? What changed?'

I need you more than ever now, she wanted to cry. *I've lost everything else.*

I can't lose you too.

'We had a good time together,' he agreed, the colour still high in his narrow cheeks, his gaze not quite meeting hers, 'but things change, don't they? People move on. That's what's happened to us.'

'You make it sound inevitable,' Jenna said miserably. 'I thought we were growing closer together.'

He'd never said he loved her. But Jenna hadn't minded. She wasn't sure she loved him either. She liked him very much. She was confident that feelings would grow and develop. What was love anyhow? How would she know when she got there? She didn't know but now she wasn't to have the opportunity to find out. William had made it very clear yesterday that it was over between them. He needed space apparently. It wasn't her, it was him. He needed 'time out'. This was put rather vaguely so she wasn't sure why he suddenly needed it or what he was going to do with this 'time' so abruptly acquired from her.

He picked up the mop awkwardly and leaned it against the counter. The mop head wasn't dissimilar to his own hair style, Jenna thought briefly. She felt a terrible urge to giggle but suppressed it. Hysteria was sure to follow.

'The thing is,' William was saying slowly, and Jenna could predict what was coming, 'I'm a bit short of cash right now. Any chance of lending me some, to tide me over until my next jobseeker's allowance comes through?'

The hysteria was building like the fizzy bubbles in a shaken bottle of lemonade. Jenna gestured helplessly at the hollowed out shop and the 'for sale' sign. She waited for William to say, I see what you mean, to apologise for bothering her, to even acknowledge that for once her situation was much more desperate and serious than his own. But no. He stood there like a doleful hound.

'Your mum?' Jenna asked faintly.

'Naw. She's run out she says, until her next pension cheque arrives. It's not like I'm not trying,' he added with an edge of belligerence in his voice. 'It's not my fault I can't get a job.'

'What about getting some training? Get a qualification in some trade or other.'

'Let's not argue about that all over again. I've managed fine in the past with odd jobs and day labour. I don't need a degree to earn a wage, do I?'

'A few years ago when the economy was booming, then no. But now, well it wouldn't hurt.' Jenna tried for the hundredth time to make him see sense.

William shrugged his shoulders under the old greatcoat. 'Are you going to give me the money or not?'

Jenna bit her lip. She fumbled in her purse and came up with a twenty. She handed it over. 'It's all I can afford. William?'

He was already on his way out the door, the crisp note tucked away in his jeans pocket. He turned as though surprised to find her still there.

'I'm leaving town. I . . . I just wanted you to know.'

So she'd made her decision after all, without knowing it herself. Her subconscious knew it was the only solution. What did she want William to do with this dramatic news? Did she hope he would run back to her, clasp her in his arms and beg her not to leave? That he couldn't live without her? There was a pause during which Jenna could smell the winter salt from the nearby sea. She'd miss that. The way the sea air pervaded everything here.

'OK,' he said. 'Keep in touch.'

She heard the crackle of her money in his pocket, then the door shut and she watched him slouch into the stiff air of the seafront and then out of sight.

What did she see in him anyway? Jenna tried to feel angry with him and failed. She was going to miss him. He had problems, goodness knows, but then again who didn't these days? The fact was William could be charming, entertaining company when he tried. They'd had some good dates where music and laughter had mingled. It was only latterly he had distanced himself as Jenna's problems multiplied. She couldn't blame him. She hadn't been much fun to be with, worried as she was by her situation.

She couldn't put it off any longer. Jenna reached for the telephone on the counter.

★   ★   ★

It rang and rang for ages. She imagined Lisette at the other end of the house, slowly moving the wheelchair to get to the receiver. But it was Shelley who answered.

'Oh, it's you,' she said coolly when Jenna greeted her. She let a silence grow on the raspy line.

Jenna gripped the phone and fought for calm. Shelley could rile her too easily. She'd learned in the past to ignore her barbs. Somehow in the intervening years she had forgotten what her stepsister was like.

'How are you?' Shelley asked emotionlessly.

'That's why I'm phoning,' Jenna said carefully. 'I'm in a bit of a fix and I need some help.'

'What on earth has happened?' There was no mistaking the lightness of her tone. There was no concern for Jenna there but a sneaking delight in her woes.

'I've lost my business, Shelley. With it, I've lost my home too. I've nowhere to go.'

'Why are you phoning here?'

She was going to make Jenna lay it all out. To make her beg for help. Well, if that was what it took, she would do it. There was no room for pride now. Jenna took a deep breath. 'Would it be OK if I came to stay? Just for a while until I sort myself out.' There, she'd said it. For one appalling moment she was sure Shelley was going to say no.

'You want to come here? That's funny. You couldn't wait to leave home five years ago. Now you're begging to return.'

Shelley was right. Jenna had been desperate back then to escape the cloying atmosphere of the Glasgow townhouse. To escape from Lisette's bitterness and Shelley's jealousy and Donna's withdrawn behaviour. She'd been mourning her father and it had all been too much to bear. Coming back to the Highlands had released her. Freed her to soar high. Only she'd crashed to earth with a painful bump.

'I'm at rock bottom,' she said plainly. 'I've very little left. You are my family. I hoped . . . '

'We do need a cleaner,' Shelley said, over the crackling connection. 'Mummy had to let the last one go — she was so lazy. I suppose you could take that on, in return for lodgings.'

Jenna heard a voice in the background at Shelley's end of the line. The line went mute as if Shelley had muffled the receiver with her palm. Then it crackled again and Lisette's sharp voice floated out of the ether to her.

'Jennifer? Are you still there? Answer me!'

Jenna winced at the use of her full given name. She hated it and had turned it into 'Jenna' as soon as she'd left home. Lisette's use of her original name reminded her strongly of her childhood and all the reasons she'd wanted to leave.

'Hello Lisette. Yes, I'm here. How are you?'

'You know how I am, Jennifer. I am always, but always, the same. I don't know why they bother with the massages, the physiotherapy. It's a waste of time. I wish your father could see me now. How he has left me.' Lisette's English was perfect but her French accent remained and a certain stilted turn of phrase.

'The accident wasn't his fault, Lisette.' Jenna blinked away warm tears.

Six years had passed since the awful road accident which had claimed her father's life and left her stepmother crippled and in a wheelchair. Lisette blamed Norman Mackenzie's driving. He hadn't seen the car coming towards them out of the mist, driving on the wrong side of the road. In vain Jenna had tried to explain that it didn't matter whether he'd seen it or not, there was no time to react before the impact. The accident had left Lisette bitter and angry at her fate. She had to blame someone. So she blamed her husband.

'You want to visit us, Shelley tells me. I can't remember the last time you did so.'

'Two years ago,' Jenna reminded her patiently. 'On my way to France, if you recall. I stayed a couple of days before going to the airport.'

'Of course. Well, you can come and stay for a short while. You will understand you'll have to contribute to the household? Shelley tells me you'll clean the house in return for a room and your meals.'

'I'm happy to do that,' Jenna agreed.

A great wash of relief flooded over her. She had a place to go.

'Very well. You may tell me when we can expect you to arrive,' Lisette said stiffly.

It was too much to hope that they would welcome her with warm hearts, Jenna decided. She had very little in common with them. Putting the phone down after explaining her travel plans, she vowed to make things better between them all. Perhaps this was an opportunity to get to know her family better and to build bridges. It would be nice not to feel so alone.

She left the shop, shutting its door behind her for the last time. The estate agent would deal with its sale now. She walked away up the windy street without looking back. An era of her life had finished and a new one had begun.

She let herself in to her terraced cottage and stood for a moment. The packing boxes had arrived. There was yet another task to be done. Somehow she'd have to find storage for her belongings. She couldn't imagine Lisette being pleased if she arrived with enough stuff for a year!

Leaving it all for now she clattered up the tiny staircase to her bedroom. Some things she would take with her. She had a framed photograph of her mother and father beside her bed. That was essential. She packed it carefully, wrapped in tissue, into her leather suitcase. She pulled open the bedside cabinet's top drawer and took out a thin bundle of letters. She was about to put them into the suitcase but hesitated. She lifted the top one and skimmed it. It was written in a round childish script with the dots of the 'i's made of open circles like little bubbles.

For some reason Donna had started writing to her a couple of years before. Shortly after Jenna's last visit home. Each letter was short and full of homely news. What Donna had been doing and what Shelley had done. Jenna was strangely touched that Donna wrote. She wrote back too, finding it an odd activity which cramped the hand and strained her imagination. Apart from running the shop, making chocolate and seeing William and Ann, there was nothing to tell. It made her realise how simple her life was. But she'd been contented until recently . . . until it had all collapsed.

A photograph slipped from the bundle and fell to the floor. She picked it up and glanced at it. Donna had included it with her most recent letter.

We were invited to a Hallowe'en party, she wrote, the bubbles above 'invited' particularly round and exuberant. On the back of the photograph she'd written only *Bennybank, October 31st*.

Jenna hadn't a clue what that meant. The picture showed Lisette sitting in her chair to the side of the photo, in front of some shrubbery. A small dog, of indeterminate breed, sat at her feet. She had a tartan car blanket wrapped around her and there was a puff of mist visible on her breath. A cold autumn day then. Somewhere. Beside her was

Shelley, boldly dressed in a lambskin coat and high black leather boots, making the most of her golden hair by winding it onto one shoulder. It cascaded gloriously, mingling with the astrakhan collar of her coat.

Donna stood beyond her, looking embarrassed to be caught on camera. Her dark brown hair merged with the shadows but her bulky shape was accentuated by a badly chosen baby-pink fleece top over a long, square cut denim skirt.

Between the two young women stood a tall man. He was strongly built like a rugby player with almost black bristly short hair and a hint of five o'clock shadow on his blunt jaw.

There was something about his brown eyes. Jenna peered at the photo. It was as if there was a message in his gaze to the camera. He called out to her from the print paper. She shook her head to clear it. She dropped the photograph on top of the other papers and zipped the case.

Soon she would lock the door of her home and deposit the keys with the estate agent. Within a few days she'd be gone from here and started on her new life in the busy city. Jenna tried on a smile to cheer herself up. It wavered and fell away. She lay on her bed and sobbed.

2

Jenna buttoned her coat right up to her neck and sheltered under its warm hood. Even her gloves weren't thick enough to keep out the chill. It was a raw day with sleety drizzle which landed and melted instantly to icy water on the skin.

She left the townhouse porch and stepped with some relief into the busy throng of shoppers on the street. The Christmas rush had begun, even though it was not yet December, and people were hurrying along, heads down against the sleet, bulky shopping bags and parcels banging against each other on the narrow pavement. It was a far cry from home. Jenna felt a sudden pang for the quiet harbour front she'd left behind.

On the news the weather man had predicted heavy snow for the Highlands. She could imagine it easily from winters past. There would be high drifts in the mountains and a thick, muffled layer on the cobbled streets. The sea would break up the carpet of snow like a great riband of pewter. It was never terribly busy in the little town with crowds. She could breathe easily there.

A sharp jab from an umbrella to her forehead made her wince and cry out in pain. The blurred figure mumbled an apology and scurried on regardless. People pushed round her rudely as she stood on the pavement. Yet it was still good to be out of the house and its brittle atmosphere. So much for her vow to improve her relationship with them all. So far all she'd achieved, it seemed, was to exacerbate the strange dynamic between Lisette and Shelley. It had started the moment she'd arrived the previous week.

She was exhausted from her journey and from organising the storage of all her belongings. An emotional parting with Ann had taken its toll too.

There was no-one to greet her at

Glasgow Central Station so she'd taken a taxi cab to her stepmother's house. It was one of a long row of elegant Victorian townhouses perched high on one of Glasgow's many drumlins. Each house had a portico of fluted columns creating a feeling of style and grandness. On one side of the townhouses was a busy main street with shops and restaurants and streams of traffic. On the other side was a long railing and beyond, a magnificent city park of lawns and tall trees and the lazy brown curve of the river. At the familiar view, she felt better. Perhaps she would be back in her old bedroom which faced the park.

She rang the doorbell but no-one answered so she cautiously pushed open the door and went inside.

'Hello?'

'So you made it.' Shelley leaned over the balcony, in no rush to join her in the hallway.

There was an electric whirr and Lisette appeared from a room beyond.

'Jennifer. I wasn't expecting you until dinner time.' A frown creased the older woman's face. She had a fine bone structure and must have been quite beautiful in her youth. Her greying hair was still thick and swept up into a French twist. Two deep grooved lines ran from her nose down both sides of her mouth, marring her looks. Whether they were from pain or discontent, it was hard to say. Her mouth was down turned and she looked displeased to see her husband's daughter.

'I'm sorry, Lisette,' Jenna heard herself say. 'I caught the earlier train by pure luck.' She could have kicked, herself immediately. She was barely across the threshold and already she'd reverted to the behaviour of her teenage years in this house. Then, she'd spent her time apologising to Lisette for everything, never able to do anything right. She'd promised herself that she'd do things differently. After all, she was now a grown woman.

Lisette sniffed, somewhat mollified

by the apology. She waved one immaculately manicured hand at Shelley, who was coming downstairs.

'Darling, show Jennifer to the lilac guest room.'

'The lilac? But Mummy, you know we'll need that if the cousins visit in the holidays. I've made up the spare room.'

Lisette's eyes were flint as she stared at Shelley. 'I specifically said the lilac room.'

Shelley paused, then she smiled at her mother and flicked her dark blonde hair gracefully from her face. Her blue eyes widened innocently.

'Did you? I can change it if you want me to.' She gave a little sigh. 'It's no bother. I can move the flowers and all the linen. I just thought Jenna might prefer a more . . . private room.'

Jenna was determined not to react. She pinned a polite smile to her lips while she waited. The lilac guest room was large and pleasant with a lovely view of the park land. She guessed that her own, original bedroom adjacent to the lilac room had been taken over by Shelley. The spare room was much smaller with a window which looked out at the back court and the wheelie bins. It was tucked away and never used. The family had never needed it.

'Oh, very well,' Lisette said, 'I'm sure you're right darling.' She wheeled herself round expertly and left the two of them standing there.

Shelley shrugged. 'You know where the spare room is. I expect you can manage your own suitcase.' She splayed her long fingers elegantly and frowned at her fingernails. They shone expensively with French polish.

'I'll take you up to your room.' A voice sounded behind Jenna. She turned to see Donna's tentative smile. 'Did you have a good trip?'

These few kind words of welcome made Jenna want to weep. What was wrong with her? She did nothing but cry these days, leaving her emotionally wrung out and hollow.

'Hello Donna. Yes, I enjoyed the

travel on the train, thanks.'

'You're tired though. Let me carry your bags.'

Shelley made a face at her sister and stalked off, her high wedge heels making harsh, stamping noises on the wooden parquet floor.

Jenna followed Donna gratefully up the stairs and along a bright, airy landing to the small spare room.

'I'm really sorry you're not in the lilac room,' Donna flushed. She fiddled unnecessarily with the plain cream curtains, adjusting them to hide the ugly view. 'I suggested it to Mum and it was all fine. But Shelley overheard and . . . ' she paused uncomfortably, 'she thought this would be better. It is more private. What do you think?'

Jenna cast about for a response. The room was adequate. Although small there was sufficient space for a single bed, bedside cabinet, wardrobe and easy chair. Besides, she was lucky to have a place to stay at all. With any luck, she'd find a job and get back on her feet within months. This was temporary after all.

'It's fine,' she told Donna firmly and was rewarded by a relieved smile.

'I'll leave you to settle in,' Donna said. 'Once you're ready, there'll be a cup of tea downstairs.'

Jenna smiled back. At least one member of the family seemed pleased to see her.

★   ★   ★

After a few days, Jenna had settled into a routine. She made breakfast for them all early as Lisette was often up by five o'clock while Shelley had to leave for work at eight. Then she cleared away the breakfast dishes and began to clean the house. She then made lunch for herself, Lisette and Donna. After lunch she was free each day to do as she wished. She decided on a week's grace before she started seriously job-hunting.

This morning had started badly,

though. She'd stumbled out of bed still fuzzy with sleep at five thirty. Her head was pounding with sinusitis from her lingering cold. In the hall downstairs there was a loud argument going on, which must have woken her. The alarm clock beeped tardily. Jenna switched it off before its irritating call could add to her headache. She pulled on her bathrobe and took a towel, intending to take a quick shower in the bathroom at the end of the corridor. As she left her room to nip along to it, she could make out the voices. It was Lisette and Shelley.

'I'm fed up doing the laundry. It's your fault for sacking Mrs Baum. Why should I have to do it?' Shelley's voice rose petulantly.

'Donna does half,' Lisette argued back, 'yet she is not complaining. Really darling!'

'Mummy, I'm serious. I've had enough.'

There was a silence during which Jenna froze guiltily at her listening post on the upstairs landing. Had they sensed her presence? Apparently not, because Shelley spoke again, softer now, coaxing.

'Mummy, darling, it's you I'm thinking of. I'd much rather be reading to you or sitting with you listening to music than wasting our precious time together sorting dirty washing. Why don't you ask Jenna to do it? She has plenty of free time.'

'She's already cleaning and making meals. Is it not too much to ask?'

'She's living here for free.' Shelley's tone hardened. 'Why shouldn't she help out?'

Jenna crept away, not wishing to hear more.

Once she was showered and dressed she headed downstairs, knowing what was coming. Sure enough, as she buttered the toast for breakfast and laid out dainty bowls of jam and marmalade on the dining room table, Shelley appeared. Lisette took her place at the table and poured tea. Donna arrived

31

with a muttered apology for being late.

'Ah, Jenna,' Shelley said nicely. 'Mummy was wondering if you wouldn't mind helping with the laundry?'

Jenna laid out the cutlery carefully before answering. She felt nauseous with her thick head and the back of her throat was scratchy. She was not in the mood for a fight.

'Of course,' she replied evenly, 'it's not a problem, Lisette, if that's what you really want.' She addressed herself solely to her stepmother, making eye contact.

The older woman caught her gaze briefly before turning her attention to the teapot. The grooves around her mouth were so deep they were like black, drawn lines.

'Mummy?' Shelley prompted softly.

'If it isn't too much trouble, Jennifer, then please. Oh, this pot, so terrible the dripping from the spout. You must use the rose china set tomorrow.'

Jenna ate her breakfast as quickly as she could and cleaned the house swiftly.

She had to escape for fresh air or she'd scream.

★   ★   ★

The jab from the umbrella galvanised her into action. She wasn't ready for Christmas shopping. She headed in the opposite direction, away from the crowds, to the back of the townhouses and a gate leading into the city park. The railings were patterned with droplets of melted sleet. Her glove was soaked just by opening the gate.

She wandered down a tarmac path. On either side of her were sweeping, sloped lawns with magnificent tall oaks and limes. Their branches were bare and rain-darkened, reaching for the iron sky. She went past a children's play area looking forlorn and deserted. It wasn't the kind of day or season for the park. Jenna stopped by the pond to watch the ducks. They were only common mallards but she admired the drakes' metallic green heads and felt

33

sorry for the drabness of the streaky brown females. A grey heron stood hunched like an old man in the shallows, waiting for a fish. Jenna stopped still. It was unusual to see a heron so close up. She wished she'd brought some bread for the birds.

A little dog ran up yapping at her and the heron flapped its large wings and flew off silently, looking for all the world like a prehistoric pterodactyl.

'That was your fault,' Jenna said to the excitable dog, trying to sound severe.

He let his tongue hang out of his mouth, grinning at her, bowed down on straight front legs, ready to play.

'You're a cute little guy; what's your name?'

'Scout? Scout?' The shout came from the far side of the river and seemed to hang in the air.

The dog's tufty ears pricked up but he made no move to leave Jenna's side.

'That answers that,' she laughed. 'You're Scout.'

He was a funny little mongrel, part terrier and part something furrier, she guessed, and wondered why he seemed familiar.

'Hmm . . . have we met before?' she asked him teasingly.

'I beg your pardon?' A deep, puzzled voice said.

Jenna spun round. Oh, my goodness. It was him! The man from the photograph. He was even more hand-some in real life. He was tall and broad-shouldered with thick, dark, spiky hair. But what made her draw in her breath was his deep brown eyes. There was such a sadness in them for a moment until he saw her staring and it was suddenly masked.

'Did you ask me something?' he said, and she detected a southern English accent, pleasant on the ear.

'I was talking to Scout,' she explained.

Scout grinned at her and wagged his tail.

'He's a great conversationalist,' he agreed with amusement.

A sudden shower made them both run for the shelter of the overhanging trees across the path. A lone squirrel scampered up the boughs, its tail stringy from the wetness.

'I wasn't expecting to see anyone else in the park today,' the man said. 'The weather's appalling.'

As if to illustrate his point, a squall of wind rose up blasting them with chilly air and slamming empty crisp packets against the tree trunks. Jenna huddled into the trees. 'Neither was I,' she shouted over the wind's howl.

'So what brings you out on such a day? I'm Gus by the way.'

'Jenna Mackenzie. Pleased to meet you. I needed fresh air.'

'There's certainly plenty of that,' he laughed.

Just as quickly, the squall subsided and a weak sunshine filtered through the dull sky.

'Scout and I were on our way to the bridge over the river to see the goosanders. Would you care to join us?'

Jenna hesitated. She didn't know this man at all apart from seeing him in a photograph. He looked strong enough to overpower her easily. She glanced about. The park was completely empty of people. Yet she felt absurdly safe with him. Perhaps it was the sadness that shone from his eyes when he forgot to hide it. Perhaps it was the fact that Scout clearly adored him and dogs are never wrong about kindness and trust. Whatever it was, she found herself nodding. She hadn't a clue what a goosander was but it didn't matter. For the first time since moving to the city she felt a little bit happy. Even her headache was better from the fresh air. A catch in her throat made her cough badly, a reminder that she still wasn't better.

Gus waited until she recovered. 'Are you OK? That didn't sound too good.'

He touched her shoulder lightly in a gesture of genuine concern. An unusual tingle went through her at his touch as if electricity had shot from him to her through the material of her winter coat.

He whistled for Scout and waited for her to catch up to his long stride. They walked together easily like old friends.

A Victorian stone carved bridge arced gracefully over the river. Jenna leaned on her elbows to look over the edge at the sluggish water below. Gus stood beside her, peering at the river, then with a shout of triumph pointed upstream.

'There they come. See them?'

All she could see were two grey birds with brown heads bobbing on the slow current along with a white bird.

'Are they goosey . . . whatsits?' she asked, trailing off as she discovered she couldn't remember what he'd called them.

Gus threw back his head with a guffaw. It was a great, hearty noise and she joined in, with Scout yapping at their feet and spinning in circles trying to nip his own tail.

God, it felt good to laugh, Jenna

thought. It was as if all her built up tension simply fell away. Right there at that very spot, right now she was happy. It was possible after all to experience that emotion. She'd imagined never being happy again. She'd learned something about Gus too. That he hid his sadness, wrapped it in layers of joviality so he appeared bluff and relaxed to the world.

'Yes, they're goosanders,' Gus said finally.

'You're a birdwatcher then?'

'Not me. My wife.'

So he was married. Jenna glanced involuntarily at his left hand. He wore a thick gold wedding band. Of course, a gorgeous man like Gus would have a significant other. There was no reason for her sudden shaft of disappointment.

Dark clouds shaded the feeble sun now and the park looked grim and desolate. 'I must be getting back,' Jenna said.

'Nice to have met you.' Gus dipped his head politely. 'Come along Scout, we should get going too.'

There was no reason to linger but she turned reluctantly in the direction of the long upward slope of the path. Where would she go now? She had no desire to shop, no wish to battle the crowds. She would have to go back to the house. She stepped out feeling her feet damp. There was a leak in her shoe. How could she afford a new pair right now? The answer was she couldn't. Not until she found employment. It was time to start looking in earnest. She decided she'd spend the afternoon doing just that. Then she became aware of footfalls and looked round. Gus and Scout were following her. There was an awkward moment as they realised they were going in the same direction.

Gus broke it first. 'I'm not stalking you, honestly. We're visiting friends up there.' He indicated the townhouses with a nod of his head.

'Oh. I live there,' she said, though she didn't have to tell him anything.

'Which number?'

She told him and he looked surprised and puzzled in equal measures.

'You're living at Shelley Linton's house? She never mentioned it to me.'

Shelley and Donna had kept their own surname when Lisette married Norman Mackenzie. Jenna remembered the first argument between her father and her new stepmother over their married name. Her father had wanted Lisette to change her surname to his, while she was adamant she would not. Lisette had won that particular battle but even as a child Jenna could see how hurt her father was by the decision, although he appeared finally to accept it. So Gus would not have made a connection when she told him her name.

'I'm Shelley and Donna's stepsister,' she explained. 'I'm staying for a few weeks.' With any luck, it would be weeks and not months. 'How do you know the family?' she countered.

'I met Shelley first and through her

got to know her mother and Donna. I should probably let Shelley tell you how we met.'

'Sounds mysterious,' she teased, feeling surprisingly at ease talking to her handsome companion.

'Not really, but unusual certainly.' He clearly wasn't going to say more. Jenna was intrigued. Did his wife know about Shelley?

They had reached the house. Before she could reach for the brass knocker, the door swung open and Shelley stood there. Her eyes were cold, blue chips as she stared at Jenna, but her smile for Gus was warm and pretty.

'Gus, how lovely. I was wondering where you'd got to. Coffee's on. Come in.'

Scout yapped excitedly, his claws clicking on the flooring as he trotted inside.

'No you don't.' Shelley looked horrified at the muddy creature. She threw another sweet smile at Gus. 'Sorry Gus, I can't help being allergic.'

'No problem. Come along old chap. I'll tie you to the porch.'

Scout let out a mournful groan but to no avail. He flopped down as the door shut him out.

'Let's go into the lounge, it's warmer in there,' Shelley suggested. As she guided Gus through, she called to Jenna over her shoulder, 'Be an angel and bring us some coffee and biscuits, would you?'

Jenna could read Shelley like a book. She'd made her point. *Hands off Gus, he's mine.*

What she didn't realise was that Jenna didn't want him anyway. Firstly, he was married. Secondly, despite the undeniable fact that he was a very attractive man, Jenna was not yet over William. Even if she was, she wouldn't blunder straight into a new relationship. If her experience with William was anything to go by, it was too complicated and draining a process. She didn't have the energy or sufficient reserves of emotion to deal with that right now. She might never have again.

Scout let out a plaintive howl. Jenna felt like joining him.

3

Gus sat sipping coffee and making conversation, outwardly relaxed, but his thoughts flew back and forth fast.

Why had he invited Jenna to join him at the bridge? That was a special ritual between, him and Leila. Oh, Leila. He missed her so much. They would walk on Saturday mornings, after breakfast, from Bennybank along the river to the bridge. Leila wore her binoculars like a necklace. There were always birds on the river. She could name them all and tell you their life cycles. How many eggs they laid, what colour the eggs were and how many broods the adults would have in a season. It never stuck in Gus's head. All he liked hearing was the sweet song of Leila's accent as she talked to him. He liked the way the sun glinted on her blonde hair making it pure spun gold. He adored her frown when she realised he wasn't learning and scolded him.

Even towards the end, they still made it to the bridge over the river. He supported her as they walked. When she grew weaker, he would half lift her so she could watch across the bridge edge. When she was gone he and Scout continued to walk there. But he had never invited another person to join them. He couldn't explain it.

He looked across at Jenna. Shelley was talking animatedly to him from the sofa opposite. Donna had joined them, sitting quietly on the armchair by the fire, content to listen. Jenna wasn't sitting with them. She was kneeling by the fireplace, placing more coals with the brass tongs. A dust rag lay beside her. Was she seriously going to polish and clean?

She was pale and thin. *Too thin*, he thought. Her grey eyes were big and wary in a gaunt face. What was wrong with her? Was she ill? His protective instinct rose up. He felt sorry for her.

Of course, that was why he'd suggested she join him to see the goosanders. Gus felt a sense of relief at having puzzled this out.

'Gus?' Shelley was asking something.

'Sorry, what was the question?'

'You were miles away.' Shelley flicked a glance from him to Jenna and back. 'I was asking you how your businesses are going.' She crossed her legs in a ladylike fashion, smoothing down her olive green pencil skirt. The length of her shapely legs was visible, clad in sheer wool. The artist in him admired her beauty. Shelley was divine, a photographer's dream. A good friend too. But nothing more.

Gus put down his coffee cup. 'Funny you should mention the businesses. I wanted to get your help with one of them. Yours too, Donna, if you don't mind.'

Donna went bright red and tugged at the cuffs of her fleece. He liked Donna. She was cursed with terrible shyness but was so kind to him and to Scout in

47

a quiet, un-showy manner. Shelley leaned forward eagerly.

'Of course we'll help. What is it? Is it the art gallery? Do you want me to show customers round? That girl Izzy isn't up to much, is she? Has she let you down?'

Gus raised his brows in surprise. 'Actually no, it isn't the art gallery. That's running well at the moment. Izzy has some new layouts planned. She doesn't need help but if you'd like to show the art to customers then I'm sure I can sort something out.'

Shelley shook her head. 'Izzy can be . . . difficult to work with. Sorry Gus, I don't mean to gossip about her behind her back but it's true. Look what she said about me last summer when I did some temping for you there. If she's there, then no, I'll keep to my secretarial temping work.' She paused.

Gus didn't say anything. He wasn't sure what Shelley meant. Izzy worked hard for him. He had no intention of letting her go to replace her with

Shelley. If she changed her mind, he'd find Shelley a position at the gallery even though he didn't need anyone else. There was a little flash in Shelley's eyes but it was gone so quickly he might have imagined it.

'It's the dating agency,' Gus said. 'In the run-up to Christmas I'd like to do something different with it. I'm not sure what, that's the problem. A gimmick of some kind?'

Surprisingly, it was Donna who answered.

'What about giving out chocolate or little pastries for all the booked dates?'

At the fireplace Jenna stopped polishing the brass log bucket and looked interested.

'Trust you to think of sweets,' Shelley said to Donna with a pointed look at her sister's stomach.

'I'd like to hear more,' Gus said, wanting to stop Jenna from cleaning and draw her into the conversation.

Donna shrugged helplessly. 'Choco-late and Christmas go together, don't they? Sorry Gus, my imagination can't take it any further. I'm not the creative type. Jenna? What do you think?'

'You could make it really special by providing handmade chocolate cup-cakes,' Jenna suggested, 'with seasonal flavouring like rum or orange. Maybe even clove and nutmeg.'

'Sounds delicious, but where would I get those made?' Gus was warming to the idea. It wasn't that his dating agency wasn't doing well. The opposite was true in fact. He had many happy, satisfied customers. It was a discreet, low-key agency for people not only looking for love but also for simply friendship and companionship. People who wanted to join were vetted carefully. The staff and customers were a loyal bunch and Gus wanted to give them a treat in some way as a thank you.

'I could make them for you,' Jenna said.

'You?' he tried and failed to keep the note of disbelief out of his voice. She looked too unlikely, kneeling there in a pair of jeans and an old jersey that had seen better days, a dust rag in her hand and a smut of coal on her cheek.

'I'm trained as a baker,' she said, tipping her chin up proudly. 'Until recently I had my own shop selling handmade cupcakes and other baking.' Her grey eyes were steady as she spoke.

'What a shame. Poor Jenna's business went bust,' Shelley added without a hint of sympathy.

Jenna seemed to shrivel. She clutched the rag but Gus wasn't going to let her off that easily.

'Lots of small businesses are going belly-up in this economic climate,' he said. 'It's tough out there. Can we chat about this some more later, Jenna? I think it could work.'

Shelley sprang dramatically from her seat. 'I've just had the most amazing idea Gus.'

They all waited while Shelley paced the floor, fingers steepled under her chin, her glorious hair swinging as she commanded the floor.

'Yes, that's it,' she announced, making sure she had their full attention before going on. 'How about a competition? How many love affairs has the agency produced? You'll provide a dream Christmas wedding to the couple who get engaged through meeting at the agency. If there's more than one such couple they'll have to battle it out somehow to win the prize. The prize could include a gorgeous wedding gown, reception and romantic honeymoon.'

'Fantastic,' Gus said. 'I like it Shelley.'

'It's a great idea,' Jenna said, unexpectedly joining in. 'I could do chocolate favours for the guests. If you wanted,' she added hurriedly.

Gus noticed how her face lit up with enthusiasm, making her unbelievably pretty. Suddenly he wanted to see her engrossed with the plan. Let her be enthusiastic. Let it bring colour to her pale cheeks. Whatever she was suffering from, it would do her good to have something to focus on.

'Yes, that'd be wonderful,' he agreed. 'Shelley, I'm going with the competition idea and Jenna, I want to employ you to make the chocolates and cupcakes. Unless you've other plans that is?'

Jenna indicated the dust rag with a wry smile. 'I'm free every afternoon so, yes please, I'd love to be involved.' Her eyes were silver with delight.

Absurdly, Gus felt pleased with himself for being the source of her obvious pleasure. He stood up, eager to start sorting out the arrangements.

'Will this competition encourage you to return to the dating scene?' he joked to Shelley.

'Shelley used to date at Gus's agency,' Donna explained to Jenna. 'That's how they met.'

'We never dated though, did we Gus?' Shelley said, unable to hide her obvious regret. 'It's a great way to meet interesting people, though. I may well go back to it. Who knows, I could even win the dream wedding. You should try it yourself, Gus. At the very least it would be a chance for you as the owner to see if it all runs smoothly. To go undercover, so to speak.'

★   ★   ★

Gus untied poor Scout who looked reproachfully at him. Luckily the dog didn't bear grudges and was soon running ahead sniffing at trees.

Gus found himself walking a familiar route. It took him from the Lintons, down through the park and once more across the river. Then he was walking in the near direction of Bennybank but before he reached the mansion house he veered right to a quiet wooded plot next to the medieval stone church.

All the way he mused on Jenna. She intrigued him. Who was she? A girl who needed feeding up, who needed some tender loving care. Hopefully that would be provided by her family now that she'd come to stay with Lisette and her daughters. What had happened to her that she was so thin and looked so tired? Why did he care anyway? Gus shook himself mentally.

He walked past the old church, struck once more by its incongruity. Its ancient stonework and peaceful garden of remembrance were backed by high rise flats. Bennybank and several other large houses were all that remained of grander days in this part of the city. The sixties and seventies had been a time of urban renewal where old properties had succumbed to the wrecking ball to make way for modern housing. He thought briefly of Thornley Estate but shut that particular door to the past firmly. Bennybank was sufficient for his needs.

'Leila my love, I've been given some great ideas to promote the business.' He stood in front of the stone angel and told his wife what he intended to do. It was calm in the church yard. The angel wore tears of recent rain. A lone blackbird sang its hurdy gurdy song to no-one. But Gus felt her presence as keenly as ever. She was in the stems of the grass, the bark of the trees, the softly soughing wind.

* * *

He'd imagined himself immunised by now against loneliness but as he busied himself in the kitchen at Bennybank, the radio blasting out tinny jazz against the relentless silence, Gus admitted it to himself. Shelley's careless suggestion came back to him. He could try his own dating agency. He wasn't looking for love. He'd been lucky, finding his own true love early in life. He rolled his wedding ring, feeling the smoothness of the metal against his skin. He'd lost Leila far too soon. Only five years together before she'd died of cancer at twenty-five. He was a widower at thirty. No, he wasn't looking for love, but would it be a bad thing to date for friendship?

An image of Jenna flashed into his head. It was daft. He knew nothing about her. She could be married for all he knew. It didn't matter to him anyway. She wasn't his type. She was too scrawny. Her hair was dark. She . . . With a sigh, Gus slid down against the breakfast bar. He rubbed his face wearily. Who was he kidding? He didn't have 'a type' he found attractive. In the five years since Leila's death, he'd had one disastrous short-lived relationship. Now that he'd given it voice, the loneliness released from its dam flooded through him. He could drown in it. Or he could beat it back. With years of experience, Gus put on his party face and reached for his mobile.

'Lesley, it's Gus. Look, could you do me a favour?'

* * *

Jenna scribbled feverishly. She could've hugged Gus for this unexpected opportunity. She had a commission to make cakes and chocolates. It staved off the need to find work for another while. She could do what she loved again.

Shelley had disappeared as soon as Gus left, muttering she was going out. Donna and Jenna had discussed the chocolates, pastries and cupcakes, the wedding dress, the honeymoon destinations and everything in between. Then Jenna had excused herself, itching to write down a list of ingredients and potential flavourings. Also a list for Gus of the equipment she would need to make the sweets.

Shelley had mentioned in passing that Gus owned a couple of local restaurants. Surely she could get space in one of their kitchens? She made a quick note to remind her to ask Gus next time she saw him.

Jenna caught sight of herself in the mirror on her bedroom wall. She had colour in her cheeks! Her eyes were shiny with excitement. She felt suddenly better than she had done in ages.

4

Jenna had settled in. She armed herself against Lisette's grumbling and Shelley's acid comments, using her cleaning duties as a time to conjure up chocolate recipes and cupcake designs in her head.

A couple of days after Gus had visited, a large box arrived at the house addressed to her. Lisette signed for it with a sour face but didn't ask what was in it. Jenna had no idea until she opened it carefully in her bedroom to discover a gleaming set of copper pans of the highest quality and a note from Gus asking if these were the sort of thing she'd need. If not, he'd added, just let him know and he'd get whatever she required.

She was touched by his thoughtfulness and how fast it was all moving. He was clearly a man of action once he'd decided what he wanted to happen. She cradled the pans, feeling excitement rise in her at the prospect of once more doing what she loved.

★   ★   ★

She was busy polishing the woodwork one morning soon after, when the doorbell rang.

'Get that please Jennifer,' Lisette called through in a commanding voice, very much the lady calling to her servant to admit visitors.

Jenna knew she should stand up to the old woman. She wasn't supposed to be a general dogsbody but that's what she was turning into.

With a tiny sigh, she put down the tin of wax and rubbed her sticky fingers on her apron before opening the door. And there was Ann, on the doorstep, looking tall and slender and beautiful. Jenna squeeled with delighted then flung herself on her friend.

'Ann, I can't believe it's you. What

are you doing here? Oh, it's so lovely to see you. I've missed you so much.'

Ann laughed, at once hugging her back tightly, then pushing her away at arm's length to scrutinise her.

'Hmmm. Do you look better? I'm not sure. A little colour in your cheeks which is good news but still way too thin. And what's with the Cinderella outfit? Are you going to invite me in out of this freezing cold air?'

'Of course. Come on,' Jenna said happily. Why was Ann here? She'd so much to ask her and to tell her. It was wonderful just to see her best friend again.

They sat in the living-room with a big pot of tea. Jenna introduced Ann to Lisette and promised to finish her cleaning later to make up the hours. Lisette wheeled away and they could hear her talking icily to the window cleaner who'd arrived to wash the outside façades.

Ann made a face. 'She's an old bat, isn't she? Sorry Jenna, I know she's your stepmother but honestly. I've seen more affection towards you from Tex, the shop cat. Before you ask, he's still feral and yes, I'm still feeding him for you.'

'Shhhh,' Jenna glanced back guiltily. 'She's not so bad. I'm lucky to have free board here and I don't mind cleaning and cooking in return.'

'They're your family,' Ann retorted, her eyebrows raised indignantly. 'They're meant to help you without expecting anything in return. If you ask me, they're a bunch of selfish, cold-hearted people. Look at you. Anyone can see you're hurting. You need looking after, not a list of chores from these — '

'Oh, enough about me,' Jenna cut in hastily. Ann had an incredibly strong view on what was right and wrong and wasn't afraid to act on it. She couldn't imagine the outcome of a confrontation between Ann and Lisette and didn't want to. 'What about you? Why are you here?'

'I'm opening another shop and it's

going to be in Glasgow. My dream is finally about to happen — it's a dress boutique, lots of gorgeous materials, rich velvets, silk ruffles, modern designs, lovely stuff. I didn't want to mention it before you left because it wasn't finalised. But yeah, it's happening. I can't believe how business is booming. It's weird but somehow I'm surfing the credit crunch. Oh . . . ' she stopped, appalled at herself. 'That was crass of me. I'm so sorry. Here's me mouthing off about expanding when . . . '

'Don't be silly. I'm truly happy for you. At least things are going right for one of us. Perhaps if I'd been sensible and sold pasties and pies instead of upmarket cakes in my shop, I'd be expanding my business too. So does this mean you'll be staying in Glasgow for a while?'

'Until the new year certainly. There's loads of paperwork to do and decisions to be made. I'm staying with my cousin Lesley in the West End. Which means, my friend, that in between all that, we can get together and have some fun.'

Ann had a look in her eye which made Jenna wary. Ann's idea of fun had got them into trouble before now. She liked to party wildly and dragged Jenna into it all too. It was through Ann that she'd met William at one particularly loud gathering in a Highland house which had ended up with people daring each other to swim in the nearby river at midnight. Jenna, an onlooker, was knocked into the river accidentally by a very drunk reveller and it was William who'd fished her out.

'How is William?' she asked Ann now. She had tried to phone him many times since arriving at the Lintons' but always got his voicemail. She left a message each time but he never returned her calls. She'd begun to wonder if he'd changed his phone. She'd emailed him too and had written two long letters but nothing came back. She didn't expect a letter, he wasn't a great one for correspondence, but he could manage a quick email, couldn't he? Just to let her know he was alright.

Ann pushed her white blonde hair behind her ears which made her look much younger suddenly, and shook her head. 'He's not good for you Jenna, you know that. He'll drag you down with him. Has done. You're better off without him.'

'I miss him. He's not as bad as you make out. He can be great company. You're always telling me to have fun.'

'Yes I am. But William's not right for you. I wish I'd never introduced you to each other. You're too giving and he's a taker.'

'How is he?' Jenna persisted. Ann was wrong. William took, yes, but he gave of himself too. He'd shared his life history with Jenna, laid his emotions bare. She'd done her best to help him work it all out. It hadn't been sorted, she admitted, because there was always more complications caused by other people messing William around. An occasional disloyal thought made her query how much of the problems were caused by the 'other people' and how much stemmed from William himself. But he was her friend so she stuck by him.

'William's fine in a William way,' Ann said cryptically. 'He came to see me looking for work recently so I took him on as a van driver.'

'That's wonderful of you,' Jenna exclaimed. 'I've been trying to get hold of him but he hasn't answered. Perhaps he's been too busy working.'

'Maybe.' Ann looked like she was going to say more, but then didn't. Instead she stood up and put her coat on, ready to go. 'Thanks for the tea. I've a meeting over in Partick in half an hour so I must rush. Oh, I nearly forgot. I've organised a bit of fun for us both.'

'A bit of fun?' Jenna echoed suspiciously.

'Yes. You need to get out and about. You can't stay in this house endlessly. You'll go mad with that old bat bossing you about.'

She should explain about Gus, Jenna

thought. She wasn't entirely stuck in the house. She felt a warm rush at imagining seeing Gus again. He shared her enthusiasm for the favours and Christmas treats she planned. He'd sent her equipment and he was going to make sure it all happened.

Ann was talking again. 'My cousin Lesley works at a dating agency. I'm free and single at the moment and so are you. So, I've booked us in for a double blind date on Saturday evening,' she finished triumphantly.

'You did what!' Jenna said, horrified.

'Don't be so fusty,' Ann said, swinging her handbag up onto her shoulder with a vigorous movement. 'It's not a serious date, it's a chance to meet new people and have a pleasant meal in hopefully interesting company. That's all.'

'Oh, I don't know, Ann. We won't know our dates.'

'Exactly,' Ann agreed. 'That's the fun part. Either we'll get along or it'll be hideous — in which case we don't ever have to see them again. It's perfect.'

'No, I'm not going.' Jenna shook her head. This was typical of Ann. She thought she was helping her by forcing her out into the world when all Jenna wanted was to be left alone to live quietly. Besides, what would William think when he heard she'd been on a date with someone else? He had to care, didn't he? Once he'd had his 'time out', she still hoped he'd come back to her.

'I'm not taking no for an answer,' Ann said. 'Here, take this.' She thrust a cream-coloured shopping bag at her friend.

Jenna took it reluctantly.

'What is it?'

'I'm lending you some clothes from the boutique for our night out. Just promise me you won't spill wine on them, that's all.' She hugged Jenna. 'You worry too much. I'll come and pick you up on Saturday at seven. It's going to be great.'

Lisette was snapping at Donna as Jenna hurried past with the bag of clothes. Donna's big face was blotchy as if tears weren't far away.

'You can do better than that,' Lisette was saying.

'But I don't want to. I like Stewart. He's kind and thoughtful.'

'He's a window cleaner. What kind of prospect is that?'

Donna didn't answer. She stumbled away from her mother and followed Jenna up the stairs.

'Is everything OK?' Jenna asked, wanting to help but unsure how to. She didn't feel she knew Donna very well in spite of growing up in the same house.

Donna tried to smile but it was tremulous.

'Just the usual arguments with Mum. It's fine.' She turned away into her room before Jenna could ask any more, closing the door quietly but firmly. Downstairs she could hear the scrape of the wheelchair on the polished wood, the wheels circling and circling and a cry of exasperation from her step-mother alone in the ground floor hallway.

★　★　★

Jenna lifted the soft folds of material and slid the dress over her head. It fell in perfect lines, accentuating her narrow waist, its hem caressing her calves. It was midnight blue velvet with a low, round neckline decorated with silver beading. The beads sparkled like tiny stars against the dusk of evening. Peeking into the bag again, she drew out a pair of dark blue evening sandals to match.

She'd washed and blow-dried her hair and brushed it until some of its old sheen appeared. Should she wear it up or down? She held it back from her face and grimaced. It made her cheek bones stand out too much. No, she would keep it simple and let her hair fall naturally to her shoulders. Despite Ann's plans, she wasn't out to impress. The only reason she was getting ready to go out tonight was because she knew if she didn't then Ann was quite capable of dragging her out ready or not. Her best friend was determined that Jenna was going to enjoy herself.

On a coat hanger in the wardrobe hung yet another borrowed item from Ann. It was a deliciously warm cream cashmere coat. She checked her make-up. It was minimal. A touch of lipstick, a light dusting of powder and a lick or two of mascara.

Jenna carefully put on the cashmere, terrified in case she marked it with her cosmetics. Her whole outfit was on loan from Ann's boutique and she estimated it was worth hundreds of pounds. She grabbed the tiny midnight blue clutch bag and she was ready. A glance in the mirror told her what she already knew. She looked good. It was amazing what a bit of war paint and some expensive togs could do.

'You'll do, my girl,' Ann said approvingly when she picked her up promptly at seven.

Ann herself looked stunning as usual. It was a tad unfair, Jenna thought, that Ann could look gorgeous even in a pair of faded jeans and an old sweatshirt let alone dressed for a night out. Her pale, glossy hair was swept up showing how graceful the column of her neck was. She wore a daring, plunge-necked crimson silk dress with fabulously high heeled platforms. It was a bitterly cold winter's night with frost glinting on the roads and pavements so she was wrapped in faux furs. Her drop earrings were like little ice crystals too.

'We're meeting our dates at Gillan,' Ann said as they folded themselves into the taxi and Ann gave the driver his instructions. Behind her Jenna caught sight of Lisette at one of the windows as the taxi began to glide away. Her stepmother's face was stone. Shelley stood by her, whispering in her ear, and

Jenna wondered what poison she was spreading.

She forgot about them as the taxi picked up speed and they merged into a city of lights and movement. Everyone was out on a Saturday night, it seemed. Office Christmas parties had begun and they passed clusters of people brightly dressed in their party gear, some merry so early in the evening.

'Are you sure this is a good idea?' Jenna asked as an attack of nerves hit her.

Ann patted her knee. 'Relax. We're going to have a great time, I promise. Do you know Gillan? Even if the company's dull, the food won't be. Lesley and I had a meal out there the night I arrived and it was delicious.'

Jenna tried hard to quell her anxiety. At this rate she wouldn't be able to swallow the food let alone taste it, for the ball in her throat. She tried breathing in and out slowly. It was beginning to relax her when all too soon they were out of the taxi and Ann was guiding her into the restaurant where an obsequious maître d' showed them to a window booth.

It was stunning, she had to admit. There was a candle burning in the centre of the table, casting a warm, yellow light onto a flower arrangement. The table linen was crisp and white while the cutlery shone pristinely. The window looked out onto the busy street so she occupied herself for a few minutes watching the passers-by.

'They're late,' Ann remarked beside her, glancing at her elegant watch. 'Points off for tardiness.'

'Are we giving points?' Jenna asked, looking horrified.

'Sure, and marks out of ten,' Ann teased. She leaned out of the booth beyond where Jenna could see. 'This might be them. Mmm, which would you prefer, fair or dark?'

Jenna didn't want either. She kept her gaze shyly on her lap, not sure what to do or how to act. She heard the brush of material as the two men manoeuvred into the booth, managing not to sweep aside the tablecloth.

Ann said a friendly hello and Jenna looked up finally — straight into Gus's dark brown eyes. Her own shock was mirrored in him. He ran a finger under his starched collar and with a jolt Jenna realised he was just as nervous as her.

'You're my date?' she said, then blushed crimson at her choice of words.

'Apparently.' His shoulders went down and he looked more relaxed as if seeing her had loosened his tension.

'You two know each other?' Ann asked with surprise.

The short, fair-haired man sitting next to Gus said, 'That puts me at a disadvantage. I'm Gareth and you must be . . . ?'

'Ann, and this is my friend Jenna.'

There was a round of introductions, then the waiter arrived to take their drinks orders and hand out menus.

In all the activity, Jenna managed a surreptitious look at Gus. He was even more handsome dressed in a smart dinner jacket with a white shirt and dark tie.

They spent the next few minutes choosing from the menus, while all the while Jenna was wondering what Gus was doing here. He was still wearing his wedding ring. Did he have a very understanding wife or was he simply a deceiver of the worst sort? Yet he had a kind, honest face. She remembered her instinctual trust of him in the park the day she arrived in the city.

Ann and Gareth were discussing the merits of grilled tuna steak over sirloin. Jenna leaned over to Gus. 'Were you dragged into this like me? Ann thinks she knows what's best for me.'

He looked a little embarrassed. 'I have to admit it was my idea. I bullied Gareth into coming with me.'

He poured them both some wine from a bottle brought by a silently efficient waiter. The candlelight bounced off his gold ring. Jenna looked away but he'd noticed her stare. He rolled the ring slowly on his finger and gave a little cough.

'I'm not married Jenna, if that's what you're thinking. I'm not here tonight cheating on my wife.'

Jenna blushed again. That's exactly what she'd been thinking.

'Leila passed away five years ago,' Gus went on evenly. 'I should really take the ring off. But I can't . . . not yet.'

'There's no reason why you have to,' Jenna said. 'I did wonder though.'

Gus laughed awkwardly. 'Because I'm on a blind date, you mean. You're right.'

Jenna took a quick gulp of her wine. It went down nicely, smooth and spicy. She took another, feeling its warming effects. Here she was, on a night out with Gus of all people. Perhaps the evening would be OK after all.

'It was Shelley's suggestion,' Gus reminded her. 'I realised she was right. It's a good way for me to get the customer experience by trying the dating myself. Call it research.'

'So Ann booked through your agency?'

Ann and Gareth had stopped arguing about fish. She joined in, 'So, you must be Lesley's boss then. I'm her cousin.'

'Lesley works at Gus's dating agency?' Jenna's head was spinning a little as the connections were made. She decided to slow down on the wine.

Gareth turned out to be a friend of Gus's from rugby practice. Jenna smiled, remembering her first thoughts of Gus when she had taken in his broad-shouldered physique. She'd been right about his choice of sport.

Gareth also knew Lesley, through Gus. He'd heard her cousin was coming to stay with her but didn't know it was Ann or who his blind date would be. Having pieced it all together, they began to eat their dinner, served exquisitely and tasting fantastic.

'Did you like the kitchen equipment I sent you?' Gus asked.

'Thank you, yes, it's perfect. I'll need a place to make the sweets though.

Lisette's kitchen is much too small.' Not to mention that she would probably have a fit if Jenna asked to use it for her own business. 'Shelley mentioned your restaurants. I wondered if I could get space in one of them?'

Gus gestured around them. 'I'd love to say yes but there isn't room here. Gillan is terrifically busy and so are the others.'

'This place is yours?' That explained the perfect attention of the waiting staff and their deference. She was a little disappointed, though. Where on earth would she get premises to work from? Would this mean Gus would find someone else to create the sweets for him?

'Hey,' Gus said softly, 'don't look so alarmed.'

She hardly heard his voice she was so conscious of the warm touch of his hand over hers. Her skin tingled. It was a pleasant sensation and she missed it when he took his hand away.

'There is another place,' he hesitated.

'Anywhere, I don't mind,' Jenna said quickly.

'Let me think about it. I don't know after all if it would suit.'

'Why don't you let me decide. You could take me there and I'll look it over,' Jenna suggested.

'No.' It came out harshly. Jenna took a sip of wine, a displacement activity, confused.

'No.' Gus repeated more softly this time.

The conversation widened out at that moment as Gareth asked Gus a question and Jenna was glad to let that particular subject drop. Somehow she'd hit a nerve but didn't know why.

They all chatted easily. Gareth was an amusing raconteur and had them all in stitches with his descriptions of things that had happened to him.

Ann quipped one-liners and it was clear to Jenna that the two of them were getting along really well. She was conscious the whole time of Gus. He too was jovial, enjoying the atmosphere and ready with a laugh or a comment at the stories. He was charming and suave and good company. At the end of the meal he insisted that it was on the house for them all.

'Should we have let him pay?' Jenna asked when she and Ann went to the ladies' room.

'Why not,' Ann said blithely. 'According to Lesley he's a millionaire. He won't notice a dent in his pocket from tonight. What do you think of Gareth?'

'He's nice.'

'Mmm, isn't he. I might see him again. What about you and Gus? He's gorgeous.'

'I don't think so. Not like that at any rate,' Jenna said hastily. 'We're friends, that's all.'

'Friends? Sure it isn't more? The way he was looking at you.'

'Gus is still in love with his wife.' As she said it, Jenna knew it was true.

'Didn't you say she died five years

ago? That's a long time for anyone to grieve and to be single, especially a handsome man like Gus.'

'I'm not interested in him like that. Besides, I'm still hoping William and I can sort out our issues.'

Jenna shut the gold clasp on her clutch bag with a snap. End of subject. Ann winked at her in the mirror. Over but not out, was the message. Ann knew to keep quiet now but she'd return to it, terrier-like, at some point. She never gave up.

'OK, let's rejoin our dates. Time for goodbyes, unless you want to go anywhere for nightcaps?'

Jenna shook her head. She was exhausted.

They took their leave of the two men in the foyer, all agreeing they should repeat the evening. Gus drew her apart for a moment.

'Will you drive out into the country with me tomorrow? I'd like to show you something.'

He wouldn't say more so she agreed,

mystified but with a flicker of content-
ment at the thought of spending
another few hours with him.

'Wrap up warm in the morning,' he
warned as he guided her into the taxi
after Ann.

Jenna hummed a Christmas carol on
the short journey home, making Ann
laugh and tease her about the effect
Gus had had on her.

But Ann was wrong, Jenna thought
sleepily as she got ready for bed. She
hadn't seen Gus roll his wedding ring.
He wasn't interested in Jenna in that
way. And she wasn't interested in him
either, she yawned. Of course, she
wasn't.

5

Jenna was wearing thick socks inside her wellingtons and her warmest cardigan under her winter duffle coat. Unfortunately the cardigan was also her oldest, with nubbed wool and a frayed cuff. But it couldn't be helped. Gus had warned her to dress warmly and soft snowflakes were falling this morning. It looked like the snow might lie. She pulled on a hat and gloves and went outside to wait.

He turned up in a large, new four by four vehicle and leaned over to open the passenger door for her.

'Hello. Thought we may need this bulldozer today, the snow's lying pretty thickly outside of town. Hop in.'

Jenna clambered up into the roomy jeep. The heating was on and the radio spilled out light melodies and seasonal songs. She wiped the window with her gloved fingers. She was beginning to enjoy the city in winter with its festive lights and busy inhabitants but she was looking forward to escaping today to the peace of the countryside. Behind her in the dog cage Scout yipped a doggy greeting and wagged his stubby tail.

'Can you manage that?' Gus asked as she tried and failed to clip herself into the seatbelt.

'Here, let me. It's new and the lock's stiff.' He leant over to help her and she smelt his clean soap scent. His jawline was shadowed with stubble. He was one of those men who had to shave twice a day. She had an impulse to feel the sandpaper touch of his jaw. Instead she drew back against her seat until he looked up and grinned. 'That's it. You're safe now. A drop of oil will sort out the mechanism before our next trip.'

'Our next trip?' she queried.

Gus expertly turned the giant vehicle on the somewhat narrow street and the engine purred. 'You're only here for a few weeks. I'm sure there are places you'd like to visit. Besides, I need an excuse to drive this thing otherwise I'll feel guilty I splashed out on it.'

'It's not exactly the car you'd want for city driving,' Jenna agreed drily.

'I've got my other car for that. But this, well, it'll be great for getting where we're going.'

'And where is that? You've been very mysterious.'

'I'd like the place to speak for itself.'

He neatly diverted her on to other topics and Jenna was forced to control her curiosity. Luckily the scenery was interesting and they pointed things out to each other as they drove along. There were some very Christmassy scenes. An old church with its spire snow covered, alone in the middle of a spread of white blanketed fields. A flock of black crows perched on a scarecrow which was wearing a coat of crystal white. A farmer on a red tractor chugging along a lane, shaking the snow from the hedgerow as the machine brushed past it.

Gus told her there was a flask of coffee in the bag at her feet. Jenna managed to pour two tiny cups as they bumped along and they shared the delicious espresso in a lay-by along with cupcakes from the bag.

'Did you make these?' Jenna asked, eating up the final crumbs from the cup cake.

'I did. Have another, I can see you like them.' Gus looked pleased.

Jenna was suddenly ravenous, a sensation she hadn't experienced in many months. *Why now*, she wondered. It's not fine dining. Here I am, sitting in a lay-by off a brown slushy road with traffic spraying up muck every time it goes by. The windows are misted up and the seatbelt's digging into my collar-bone. The air had a faintly doggy smell as Scout's fur warmed and dried. She was wearing her oldest, most comfortable clothes and no make-up. Yet she felt vibrantly alive. And starving!

'I will have another,' she said. 'You don't need me to bake for your competition. I bet you could make them yourself, if they are anything like these!'

Gus had another one too and they gave the last one to a grateful Scout.

'Thanks, Gus,' Jenna said. It came out sounding too serious. She wasn't sure what she meant anyway.

'It's only a cupcake,' Gus said, his eyes twinkling. 'Come on, let's get going. It's another ten minutes or so from here.'

With a sense of anticipation, she sat forward and popped the picnic things back in the bag.

Before long Gus swung the jeep right, away off the main road and out onto a quiet lane muffled with snowfall. There were late berries, incongruously scarlet, dripping from the trees at the edges. A great flock of redwings were feeding greedily on them, squabbling amongst themselves. They fluttered and rose up as Gus and Jenna drove by, giving them a glimpse of the birds' white eyebrows and russet underwings.

The lane narrowed further still and they came to a crossroads. Gus took another right and they curved round a bend and up between a pair of grand stone entrance pillars, beside which there was a beautiful old gatehouse. Jenna held her breath, mesmerised. Later she would remember her first view of Thornley House. In fact, she would never forget it.

They went up a long, sweeping driveway protected by limes. The trees' bony branches were black and stark in the winter but Jenna could imagine how lush and shady they would be in a hot summer. Ahead of her, grey and sombre against the white background, stood a house. It was a great, simple square of stone, no fancy turrets or gothic twists but something in it cried out to her. The windows were dark and empty and the place was still. It was as if the house was suspended in time. Waiting to come alive.

Gus parked in front of the main door. When the engine turned off there was nothing but silence for a moment. As if realising that, Gus cracked open his door and called heartily to Scout. Scout's barks, begging to be set free, broke the spell. Jenna too got out, feeling the stiffness in her legs from sitting for an hour.

'What is this place?' she called.

Gus appeared from the boot with Scout, setting him down to explore. 'This is Thornley.'

She followed him up the stone steps to the house, only mildly surprised when he flourished a set of keys and proceeded to let them in.

A damp, musty smell flowed over them and there was enough chill in the damp air for Jenna to keep her coat buttoned.

'The heating should be on,' Gus called over his shoulder.

'Doesn't feel like it,' she said under her breath.

Scout gave a little woof of agreement. He scampered off after Gus. Jenna increased her speed too. Just how long was this hallway? She found Gus standing in a vast living-room, staring out the window onto what may have been lawns and flower beds under the coverlet of snow.

He stood frozen like a statue. Jenna hesitated. It felt like intruding, he was so very still. Then he spoke without turning, sensing her presence. There was a note of such sadness in his voice that she shivered.

'This was Leila's favourite house.'

Jenna couldn't help it. She ran to him and hugged him as a friend, wanting to absorb some of his sorrow, to draw it out of him and then pour it away.

He clutched at her like a drowning man, burying his face in her hair. She felt his body warmth, his clean male essence, the graze of his stubble on her cheek. Then as her senses changed and she became aware of him, he drew away with a ragged breath.

'Sorry,' he said. 'A weak moment. I'm alright.'

'Why did you bring me here?' she asked. 'If it's so painful for you . . . '

Gus shook his head. 'I had no idea it would still affect me so much. It was always Leila's place, never so much mine. Bennybank, my townhouse, is less . . . complicated than Thornley.'

Jenna wondered what that meant.

'Do you want to go?' she asked.

'No, no. We've only just arrived. I'm fine now. There are kitchens here. I thought you could use them.' His voice was back to normal and his smile was ready enough.

Jenna nodded. She would play along. If Gus didn't want to discuss his innermost feelings with her, that was OK. After all, they hardly knew each other.

Even as she told herself that, Jenna knew she was wrong, on her part at any rate. She felt she had known Gus for a long, long time, she was so at ease, so comfortable with him.

'Was this the place you mentioned last night?'

'Yes, that's right. Thornley came to mind immediately. But then I wasn't sure if I wanted to come back here.'

'How come the heating's on?' Jenna asked, to distract him and lighten the atmosphere.

'Alice and Grant Russell look after Thornley for me. It's minimal, a bit of maintenance, keeping the pipes from freezing and organising gardeners for the formal gardens. We'll pop in on them before we leave. They know we're here.'

Jenna looked about at the damp stained wallpaper and the dusty cob-webs in the nooks of the ornate ceilings.

'Alice and Grant are getting old.' Gus followed her gaze. 'As I said, the maintenance is minimal. It's obviously getting too much for them.'

'This house could be lovely,' Jenna breathed. 'It is lovely.' She was entranced by the discovery of portraits above the staircase and an inglenook by the hall fireplace.

'We used to have parties here,' Gus said.

'I can imagine that. It would be wonderful with the house all lit up and big fires roaring in the hearths. It needs a party.'

'It needs something,' he agreed. 'I was going to sell it but . . . I don't know.'

'Oh, don't do that. Not yet, I mean. It's none of my business but wouldn't this be the perfect setting for your Christmas wedding competition? The winners would have their wedding reception here. There'd be light and noise and company again.' She rushed the words out before he could react and tell her it was nonsense. But he didn't.

'OK. Let's do it.'

'What?'

'I've got a media company lined up to produce a local TV advert for me. It'll be a mock wedding scene to encourage people to sign up to the agency and to the competition. They could use Thornley as a backdrop.'

'Fantastic. Especially as it's the real prize. The advert would be a taster of what to expect.'

Gus smiled at her obvious enthusiasm. For once his dark eyes had lost their sorrow and were shining, warm and alive.

'Shelley would be great as the bride in the advert,' Jenna said. She sensed Shelley wouldn't be too happy at being left out of all Gus's plans for his agency and for Thornley. This way Shelley would be centre stage for part of it at least. Just the way she liked it. Perhaps too, it would ease Jenna's relationship with her. They were half-sisters. They should be friends.

'Great idea,' Gus agreed. 'The camera loves Shelley. She's stunning.'

Jenna's stomach twinged briefly. Why did it matter if Gus thought Shelley attractive? She was beautiful and he was a man. He couldn't fail to notice. Besides Gus and Shelley were friends long before Jenna arrived to stay. It had nothing to do with her whether it was friendship or something deeper.

'That's sorted then,' Gus said, oblivious. 'I'll open Thornley up, get the place revamped. With sufficient teams of cleaners and decorators it won't take long.'

That was the power of money, Jenna supposed. Everything was possible. She felt a flicker of excitement at the thought of Thornley House restored to glory. How marvellous it would look. She couldn't wait.

Gus was taking them downstairs now to the kitchens where Jenna would work to perfect her treats. It was cold and damp one floor down and it was clear no-one had used the kitchens for a long, long time.

'We used to make some great meals here,' Gus said. 'Leila and I. We had a cook but we liked to concoct menus ourselves occasionally. It's relaxing, isn't it, to cook and sip wine?'

Jenna nodded. 'What was she like?' she added softly.

'She was bright and beautiful like a song,' Gus said without hesitation. 'Full of curiosity and full of life. How ironic for a person so bursting with vitality to be snatched so suddenly before she had a chance to experience it all.'

'I'm so sorry,' Jenna said inadequately. For what could she say? Nothing would do. But Gus surprised her by reaching out and taking her hand to squeeze it gently.

'Thank you for asking about her. No-one dares to say her name to me. My parents, when they were alive, never mentioned Leila in case I crumbled before their very eyes. Gareth too. He was friends with Leila of course but it's as if she never existed. I don't blame him. I was a mess for a long while. But . . . now I'm stronger.'

She felt the warmth and strength of his fingers on hers. A pulse of pure electricity shot through her at his touch. Confused, she gently disentangled her hand from his. She searched around for something to say to diffuse the moment.

'How soon could I start using the kitchens?'

Gus made a pretence of scratching his head and focusing on the units in front of them. 'Next week? I'll have the place ready and my chauffeur can bring you over each day.'

'Oh,' Jenna said. 'I clean the house for Lisette each morning and make meals. I won't have as much time as I'd like.'

'Lisette has you cleaning?'

'In return for lodgings,' Jenna explained sheepishly. It still didn't sound good.

'That's no use. I'll offer her my cleaner at no expense. Whatever it takes. It's more important for you to bake,' Gus said decisively.

The door behind them creaked open, making them both jump. A tiny wizened woman stood there, well wrapped in an ancient waxed jacket and gum boots.

'Alice, we were going to call in on you,' Gus said, smiling.

'Saved you the trouble then,' Alice

Russell said, her bright eyes darting up and down as she assessed Jenna. Whatever she saw must have satisfied her for she held out a wrinkled paw to be shaken.

'I'm Alice, Gus's housekeeper. You must be Jenna. You needn't look astonished, dear, Gus mentioned you and now I know why.'

Gus coughed. Jenna felt herself go red. What had Gus said about her?

Alice Russell sighed. 'I'm so pleased you're going to use Thornley again, Gus. Some of it will need more than a clean and a polish, I'm afraid.'

'How did you know what I'd decided? Until I got here today I was considering selling it after Christmas.'

'You won't sell Thornley,' the old woman said with certainty. 'Too many good memories . . . and more to be made.' The last comment encompassed Jenna too. 'I'll leave you to it but hope to meet you again dear,' she finished with a friendly nod.

They heard her footsteps, slow and

unsteady up the stairs, fading away.

'She needs more help here,' Gus said. 'I feel guilty I haven't organised it before now. Grant's even older than Alice.'

'Shouldn't they retire?'

'They should but they won't hear of it. They've looked after Thornley since my father's day. It'll take an extraordinary amount of tact for me to suggest extra help.'

'Are you blessed with tact?' Jenna asked him teasingly.

He shot her an odd look.

'What is it?' Jenna ran a hand through her hair. Was there a cobweb or worse still, a spider, in it?

'You looked beautiful last night. I meant to tell you,' Gus said. His brown eyes met hers.

Jenna laughed nervously. 'Beautiful? That's an exaggeration surely.'

'I mean it. Your hair shone copper in the candlelight and your skin glowed. You looked so much better than the day I first met you.'

I feel better too, Jenna realised suddenly. She hadn't coughed all day.

'You're trying to tell me I looked healthier rather than beautiful,' she joked.

Gus took a tentative step forwards and Jenna, unthinking, took one back. She wasn't ready for this. Before she could think it through and decide Gus didn't mean anything by it really, there was a sharp crack of splintering wood and her right foot went through the floorboard. Jenna screamed. This time Gus took more than one step forward. He grabbed at her, holding her up as she staggered to regain her balance. There was a terrible throbbing pain in her ankle. She clung to Gus, feeling his height and solid strength.

'It's OK, I've got you. I'm going to get your foot out. This may hurt a little.'

Gingerly he broke away small flakes of the rotten wood. Jenna winced. Her ankle was incredibly tender. The skin was puffy and reddened. Gus worked carefully removing the wood gradually until she was able to lift her foot free. She leaned into him unashamedly. It felt good.

'That looks nasty. I think it's sprained,' Gus said. 'Let's get you home.'

Jenna started to limp, holding him as a support but her injured foot would bear no weight.

'There's nothing for it,' Gus said and swept her up effortlessly into his arms.

Jenna protested feebly but she had to admit to herself it felt safe, so safe, against Gus's broad chest.

'You weigh nothing,' he told her, almost angrily. 'I can easily carry you to the jeep.'

Jenna let him. There was a moment of loss as he set her down gently into the passenger seat and clipped her belt. He locked Scout in the dog cage, swung himself in and Thornley House retreated until the bend in the driveway and it was gone.

I'll be back soon, Jenna promised silently.

Jenna was resting in the living-room with her bandaged foot propped up on a stool later that evening, when Gus phoned. Lisette had been surprisingly kind when Gus brought her back. Donna had bandaged her foot and Shelley, no doubt because of Gus's presence, made a big deal of bringing her a tray of food. It was a relief just to sit and do nothing that would bump her poor foot.

When the phone rang, Shelley picked up. 'It's for you. It's Gus,' she said to Jenna. She passed the handset over.

Lisette was reading by the fireside. Shelley had been sitting with her, flicking idly through fashion magazines. Jenna had dozed, sleepy with the painkillers Lisette had given her. She didn't want them listening in on her conversation but she was helpless.

'Jenna,' Gus's warm tones filled the room. 'How are you?'

The handset was on loudspeaker but

she didn't know how to change it back to one-to-one mode. Shelley smiled slyly.

'I'm comfortable, thanks.' There was no way she'd ask Shelley for help in changing the phone setting. She was sure she'd set it deliberately to hear what Gus had to say.

'I'm glad you like Thornley,' Gus went on.

Shelley's face was thunderous as she pretended to read her magazine.

'I was wondering . . . ' he paused so long Jenna was about to ask if he was still on the line. 'I was wondering if we might repeat our date?'

When she in turn didn't answer, he went on. 'Purely for research purposes, of course. We'd book through Lesley and try a different restaurant, not one of mine. What do you think?'

Purely for research. What else? She didn't want a real date with Gus anyway. She had William after all. But she wasn't thinking of William right then. She was remembering Gus's warm embrace and his tenderness while extracting her foot from Thornley's rotten floor.

'I'd like that,' she said. There was no harm in it. She'd be helping a friend, pure and simple.

'I'll bring crutches,' Gus promised. 'We'll take it easy.'

They set a time to meet the following evening. Shelley glowered but said nothing. Jenna was too tired to explain. She wasn't trying to replace Shelley. Lisette took off her reading glasses and wheeled from the room.

She couldn't help it. She was looking forward to tomorrow evening and Gus's company.

6

Her ankle was throbbing but it was bliss to be able to rest it on a footstool and sit with a notepad and pencil scribbling recipe ideas. Gus must have spoken with Lisette about her cleaning duties because there was no mention of that this morning. Instead Donna had been ordered by Shelley to bring Jenna breakfast. A Mrs Kellar had arrived shortly afterwards and began to vacuum around the house. So Jenna sat nibbling toast and honey, sipping tea and conjuring up tastes and textures for the agency goodies.

★　★　★

Ann breezed in mid-morning to visit her. She was carrying an assortment of bags and the tip of her nose was red from the cold. She plonked down on the armchair with a sigh of relief.

'It's crazy out there. I was jostled, if you can believe it, by an eighty year old for the last Santa stocking in the shop.'

'I haven't started my Christmas shopping,' Jenna grimaced. 'Not likely to now until my foot feels better.'

'How is it? Poor thing. Still, Gus was there to save you. What a hero.' There was a wicked gleam in Ann's eyes.

'Shhh,' Jenna whispered, waving her hand in agitation. 'Don't mention Gus or Thornley please.'

'Why ever not?' Ann batted her hand away as if it was an annoying fly.

'Because Shelley's furious with me,' Jenna hissed. 'She wanted to be invited to Thornley by Gus.'

'Well, well. That is interesting. I must meet Shelley, so I can assess the competition.'

'There is no competition. Shelley's made it quite clear where her affections lie and I'm not trying to oust her. I like Gus as a friend, that's all.'

'What about Gus? Doesn't he get a say in this?'

'Gus is . . . wrapped up in himself emotionally,' Jenna said, trying to explain it clearly. 'I honestly don't think he's noticed Shelley's advances.'

There was a musical bleep and Ann dived for her handbag. She rummaged in a froth of hankies, pens and perfume and came up with her mobile. She frowned.

'That's yet another text from Cammie. Your William is causing her a ton of headaches.'

'What's he done?'

'It's what he's not done that's the problem. He's very unreliable. I can't have that. I'm running a business. I need my van driver to deliver goods on time to customers.'

'Oh, give him another chance, please Ann. He needs that job,' Jenna pleaded.

'You're far too soft. In fact you're too . . . nice.'

Jenna laughed. 'You can't be too nice. Besides we all want the best for our friends, don't we?'

'What if what's best for me isn't best for William?' Ann asked.

'Give him a warning, can't you? I'm sure he hasn't realised the effect he's had.'

'This is very much a last warning.' Ann jabbed at the text buttons. 'There, Cammie will no doubt be back in touch soon.'

Jenna eased her foot off the stool. 'Was there any message for me from him?'

'You've reminded me, there was.' Ann dug into her pocket and pulled out an envelope. She passed it over with a wry twist of her mouth. 'He didn't want to pay postage so he gave it to Cammie who sent it down with the courier service.'

Jenna took it eagerly and slipped it into her own pocket. She'd read it later alone.

The door was flung open, startling them both. Shelley swept in. She was wearing a long cream dress thick with frothy tulle and a delicate embroidered bodice. Her long dark blonde hair was coiled in a clever, careless twist to the side of her head. She was made up with pink lip gloss, blue eye shadow and glittering rouge accentuating her cheek-bones. Jenna and Ann stared. Shelley pranced in to the centre of the room, her skirts rustling.

'There, what do you think?' Her face was flushed with triumph. 'I'm going to be the bride in the advert Gus is making about the agency. He's told me I'm perfect for it.'

She curved her lip with a sly look at Jenna.

'Wow, that's fantastic,' Jenna said, not wanting to spoil Shelley's moment by telling her she already knew and not only that, had made the suggestion herself to Gus. That wouldn't be fair. If she was going to improve her relation-ship with Shelley she would have to ease her way forward, gently.

'Who are you?' Shelley asked Ann rather rudely.

Jenna quickly introduced the two young women to each other.

'You look great,' Jenna said honestly.

'You bet I do. You have to work at it you know, Jenna, to look like I do. Gus appreciates it.'

Jenna carried on gamely. She ignored her stepsister's implied criticism and the innuendo that she hadn't worked on her looks like Shelley.

'Thornley'll be a wonderful backdrop for the advertisement, won't it? It's such a marvellous place. You'll love it, I'm sure.'

But she'd put her foot right in it. Shelley's face darkened at the mention of Gus's country house.

'You know fine well I haven't been invited there yet. You just want to rub my nose in it. Let me tell you something Jenna Mackenzie. I'll have the last laugh when I'm mistress of Thornley and you're still struggling to pay your way with your pathetic baking.'

She rushed past an astonished Jenna.

Ann's jaw dropped. They heard the stomp of her shoes and the distant raised query from Lisette. Then silence. Ann let out a whoosh of air.

'That's Shelley,' Jenna said lightly. Her hands were trembling from her stepsister's outburst. She interlocked her fingers until they stopped.

'She's lovely,' Ann said. 'Lovely like a python. What is her problem exactly?'

'She wants Gus. It's as simple as that.'

'I'm not so sure. Yes, she covets Gus or at least Gus's money. But there's more to it than that. No, it's you she's reacting to.'

'We've never got on, even as kids,' Jenna confessed. 'She was very unhappy when Lisette married my father and she resented me coming to live with them.'

'What happened to her own father?'

'He ran off when she was very small. I don't think she had, or has, any kind of relationship with him.'

'Did she get along with your dad?'

Jenna thought about it, casting her

mind back through the years to those darker days. She had been ten when her own mother died and thirteen when her dad remarried to Lisette. Likewise Shelley was thirteen. It was a difficult age, full of changes both mental and physical anyway, without the added burden of a newly made up, and largely unwanted, new family. At first Shelley had been completely obnoxious to both of them but gradually she'd warmed to Norman Mackenzie, eventually treating him like a father. It was Jenna she'd reserved her nastiness for. The only person Jenna felt loved by in the family was her dad. He made her feel special and told her every day how much he loved her. She tried to convey this scenario now to Ann. Ann frowned.

'Well, using a bit of pop psychology I'd guess she's jealous of you.'

'Jealous, of me? Have you seen the way she looks? She's beautiful and confident, things that I most definitely am not. No, you have to be wrong Ann.'

'Look at it again Jenna. She's

thirteen, a vulnerable age. Her dad ran off when she was a toddler making her feel unloved. She gets another father who's great but who makes it perfectly obvious that his own child is number one. No wonder she's insecure.'

'Oh, but Dad wouldn't . . . ' Jenna trailed off.

Norman had made it clear she was the apple of his eye. He had done it to reassure Jenna after his new marriage and the move to a new house. She'd never thought how that would affect Shelley or Donna. It didn't seem to have done Donna any damage. She was by nature placid and accepting. But Shelley was a different matter. Looking at it now from an adult perspective, Jenna could see what her father's behaviour had done. He'd had the right intentions but they had had unexpected consequences.

'Poor Shelley,' she whispered, aghast.

'Understanding her behaviour is one thing. Condoning it is quite another,' Ann said with asperity. 'Being horrid

when you're thirteen is sort of accept-
able, if unpleasant, but as an adult? I'd
say get over it!'

'She hasn't though, has she? She still
hates me. What can I do to change it?'
Jenna asked. 'I'd like for us to be
friends.'

'No idea.' Ann's burst of insightful
psychology was over. 'Got to go, hon.
The business won't run itself. I'll be in
touch.' She gave Jenna a hug and
gathered up her Christmas shopping to
go. 'I'll let myself out.'

★ ★ ★

William's letter was short. His hand-
writing sprawled across a grubby sheet
of paper torn from a jotter. Jenna
excused it by deciding he was too busy
in his new job to sit down and write to
her properly.

Dear Jenna,
   *How's things? Ann tells me you're
working again. Good news. She's a*

mean cow to work for. Does nothing but moan at me. I'll probably ditch the van driving soon. Might come and visit you. William.

She was pleased that he might visit. It would be good to see him. Maybe it was the chance they needed to set things right between them. For some reason she thought of Gus. What would he make of William? She couldn't imagine two more different men. Gus was self-contained and self-made, a millionaire and a successful business-man. He had cared so tenderly for her when she sprained her ankle. A prickle of pleasure ran along her spine as she remembered leaning in against him as he carried her to the jeep. She felt guiltily disloyal to William. He had his good points too. If he didn't act as a chivalrous knight to her it was because he had so many problems of his own. He needed her in a way that Gus didn't.

A little wave of tiredness washed

through her bones. It was hard not to get dragged down by William's complicated life sometimes. She should phone him up. Tell him not to give up his job for goodness sake. He wasn't likely to get another in such a small town. How long would he stay visiting? Would Lisette allow him to stay here? How would Jenna afford to pay for his board and food on top of her own? He had written that she was working again. What he didn't know was that she had yet to start. Blast her leg! Whether it was better tomorrow or not she would begin. Christmas was getting ever closer; there was no time to delay.

She tucked William's letter away and struggled to her feet. She could at least help to prepare lunch. She doubted Mrs Kellar was employed as cook as well as cleaner. It would save Lisette the bother.

'Jennifer, there you are.' Lisette's wheel scraped the door jamb as she entered, making her wince. Her jaw was taut in its usual stressed position.

Jenna's heart went out to her. It must be awful to be caged in a metal contraption every second of the day. Her clumsy entry had annoyed her. Her chagrin was there for all the world to see before she got her emotions under control once more.

'What is it Lisette? I was just coming to help make the lunch,' Jenna said. She took the weight off her injured foot, feeling it throb painfully.

'Sit, for goodness sake, sit girl,' Lisette said impatiently.

Jenna sat. She rubbed her bandaged ankle and prayed that Gus would remember the crutches. Lisette waited. She drummed her fingernails on the wheelchair armrests.

'Sorry,' Jenna said. She was always sorry. When would she learn that she couldn't please her stepmother?

'I'll come straight to the point Jennifer dear.' Lisette's eyes were like chips of pale ice. 'You've been seeing a lot of Gus Stanton since you've arrived. I know there's no intention of anything on his part but I don't want you to get the wrong impression.' She paused and smiled. It didn't reach her eyes or warm her expression. 'You see there's an . . . understanding between Gus and my Shelley. It hasn't been announced as yet but I expect it will be soon. There'll be an engagement and probably a summer wedding. Shelley deserves a position in life as Gus's wife. She'll be an asset to him, a gorgeous wife on his arm at business functions and a wonderful hostess for his business dinners.' She let slip a tiny sigh. It was plain that the match suited not only Shelley but her mother too. Jenna wondered if Gus knew what they had planned for him. He didn't act like a man in love around Shelley.

'Gus hasn't mentioned it,' she said.

'Why should he tell you?' Lisette snapped. Her chair whirred like an angry insect as she spun round to face the window and away from Jenna.

'I heard you on the telephone yesterday arranging to meet Gus. To

have a 'date' with him. You will phone
him and tell him you're cancelling.'

It was an order, brooking no
argument. Jenna was taken back to her
teenage years, hearing Lisette's brittle
tones. She had ruled with an iron will
back then.

'It's not a real date,' she said quietly.
'I'm helping him out, that's all.'

'I'm well aware of that. He has no
interest in you,' came the dismissive
reply. 'However it's upsetting Shelley so
you will do as I ask.'

'And if I don't?'

There was a snort of disbelief. The
chair glided across the floor only to
pause at the exit.

'You will Jennifer. You will.'

*　*　*

Later in the afternoon Jenna was resting
again. She'd forced herself to move
about, hobbling slowly round the
ground floor, unwilling to attempt the
stairs to her room until she absolutely

had to. She had also spent a couple of hours designing her lovers' cupcake decorations until they pleased her.

Soon she would have to get ready to go out for the evening with Gus. A flicker of defiance at Lisette's command had hardened into resolve. She was no longer a teenager, afraid of her stepmother's wrath. She was an adult. She was doing no wrong seeing Gus. It was perfectly innocent. She suspected that Shelley's 'engagement' was all in her mind. Gus would've told Jenna otherwise. He was a decent, honourable man. Ann had told her she was too nice and she had denied such a thing was possible. Maybe Ann was right. She was a doormat if she let Lisette boss her about.

Donna broke her train of thought by arriving with a steaming mug of milky cocoa.

'This is for you. I thought it might help your painkillers slip down more easily.'

Jenna reached for the capsules and

took the mug gratefully. 'This is my last lot. I'm sure tomorrow I'll be fine.' She grinned up at Donna then froze. Donna's face was pale and tear-tracked. 'What's the matter? Here I am rambling on about myself when you've worse problems than me.'

'It's Mum. She's on the warpath today.' Donna sat down beside Jenna.

'That's my fault. She's annoyed with me,' Jenna said.

Donna nodded. 'She wants you to stop seeing Gus. It's crazy. Gus is a lovely guy but he's not interested in Shelley. Mum's got herself all wound up about the two of them, it's a kind of fantasy. As for Shelley . . . I don't think she loves Gus.' She sounded guilty at even voicing this but continued, 'She wants to be Mrs Stanton and to be rich. She told me as much. Poor, poor Gus.'

'Gus will see through her,' Jenna said, more confidently than she felt. Gus was vulnerable. He wasn't over Leila. Shelley could hurt him further. It made her suddenly more determined to see him this evening. She could protect him. Somehow.

Donna was speaking again, the words spilling out like unstoppable sand in a timer.

'It's Stewart . . . I'm in love with him and he loves me back. But Mum won't hear of it. She says he's got no prospects and that I can do better. But I don't want to do better, Jenna. I want Stewart. Now she's forbidden me to see him.' She ended on a broken sob.

'Is he the window cleaner?' Jenna asked. She remembered a heavy set young man with, fair hair and ruddy cheeks puffing as he carried a set of ladders and a pail and sponge pole.

It was ridiculous of Lisette. Donna was twenty three years old. She wasn't a truculent teenager to be ordered about.

'You don't have to do as Lisette says,' she told Donna. Her own resistance to Lisette's control was widening. 'If you love Stewart you should fight for him. Of course you should see him.'

'It's not that simple,' Donna sighed,

wiping away tears. 'While I'm living under this roof I have to live by Mum's rules.'

Jenna could quite imagine Lisette saying that.

'Move out then. Go and live with Stewart,' she suggested boldly.

Donna shook her head.

'Stewart lives at home with his parents. He's saving up for a place of his own but it won't be for a while. As for me, I don't have a job so I can't afford to move out.'

'You should stand up to her,' Jenna yawned. She was drowsy of all a sudden. She drained the last of the cocoa and yawned once more.

★ ★ ★

Gus dressed carefully for dinner with a happy anticipation at seeing Jenna again.

He hummed as he adjusted his black tie in the mirror and winked to his reflection. The face looking back at him

124

was a relaxed, contented one. It wasn't a real date but in some ways that made it better. There were no nerves involved, no anxiety that he might say the wrong thing and put his date off. With Jenna he simply felt . . . good.

He turned over again in his mind that single moment in the kitchen at Thornley. What had he been thinking? The answer was, he hadn't been thinking at all. It had been pure instinct to move towards her. She had looked so appealing standing there, her large grey eyes merry from lightly teasing him, a faint pretty flush on her cheeks and her dark hair shining so that he longed to reach out and touch it. To touch her. To stroke the soft skin of her cheekbones. To kiss her full lips.

Gus stilled. He put down his cuff links before he dropped them. He had wanted to kiss Jenna. He still did. His attraction to her had built up slowly but powerfully since he met her. Gus shrugged on his dinner jacket. He checked his appearance in the mirror. A small wash of nervousness engulfed him. He couldn't deny it. It was a date after all . . . on his part at least.

Lesley had organised the booking at a small family run restaurant down by the riverside for the date. It had been established there before the renewal of the Clyde and the rocketing price of building. Now it nestled between modern glass fronted casinos and brash, expensive eateries, facing the super-expensive desirable riverside apartments.

Gus found a space in the crammed car park and went in to a welcoming atmosphere of baked garlic bread, yellow candlelight and red checked tablecloths. He looked for Jenna and did a double-take. There was no Jenna but Shelley sat at a window table. She gave a little wave. He went over to her, puzzled.

'Hello. What a coincidence. Are you waiting for someone? I'm eating here tonight too.'

Shelley smiled.

'I'm waiting for you Gus. Jenna couldn't make it so I thought I'd come instead so we didn't let you down.'

Gus's disappointment was immense. He admitted to himself then and there just how much he'd wanted to see Jenna and spend the evening chatting to her.

'You don't mind, do you?' There was an edge to Shelley's casual enquiry.

'No, of course not. It's for research, it wasn't a date,' Gus said swiftly, not wanting to upset her. It was kind of her to step in at short notice. 'You look fantastic,' he added truthfully.

Shelley flicked her hair back with satisfaction. She did look great in a mulberry wool dress teamed with knee-length leather boots. Gus sat and they ordered from the menu. When the wine arrived he poured them both a generous glass. Shelley leaned towards him cosily.

'This is nice. Just the two of us,' she breathed. She reached out and covered his hand with hers. 'We could make it a

127

real date, if we want.'

Gus extricated his hand gently but firmly. It was odd but Shelley's beauty did nothing for him. He liked her, but physically there was no magnetism. It was ironic that only days ago he'd promised himself to get out, to dissipate his loneliness by meeting people and using his own dating agency. He could take Shelley up on her offer. But it wouldn't be fair on either of them. Not now when he realised he wanted only Jenna. Whether she was attracted to him didn't matter. He had to try.

'I like you Shelley. I consider you a friend,' Gus said, 'but we wouldn't make a good couple.'

'Why not?' Shelley asked. She'd finished her wine and poured another. 'We're both good-looking people. I could be a help to you. We could have fun together at Thornley — entertaining, going travelling . . . ' she stopped and waited.

Gus was taken aback. Shelley appeared to have run the gamut from a single date right through to a serious relationship in one wishful breath. But before he could let her down gently, she was talking again, loud and shrill.

'It's that Jenna Mackenzie, isn't it? She's bewitched you. She's hardly been here three weeks and she's got her claws into you. Well, let me warn you about her Gus. She's not the sweet little girl you think she is. She's a gold digger like Kate. She wiped out her boyfriend William's money after she ran her own business into the ground. You can ask Ann if you don't believe me. Yes, ask Ann about William's circumstances.'

Shelley caught up her coat and bag and stormed past him before he could stop her. Gus sat stunned. The waitress tactfully removed Shelley's place setting and poured him more wine.

Gus drank it without tasting it. He looked out at the harbour, pretty in the night with the colourful lights of the boats and buoys. He hadn't handled this well. He'd upset Shelley by rejecting her. He knew she was moody by nature but her anger tonight had shocked him. Then she'd mentioned Kate. What a can of worms. After his disastrous short-lived relationship with Kate, he'd confided in Shelley. It was what had cemented their friendship.

He'd trusted Kate. She was his first relationship after Leila. He hadn't loved her but he'd found her attractive and charming. She'd asked to borrow money and he'd been glad to help. Gullible fool that he was. She'd stolen tens of thousands from him, disappearing in the night without a trace. He had let her go. He hadn't contacted the police. The situation was distasteful enough without an investigation and the inevitable publicity that would follow.

Gus paid for the meal he hadn't eaten and made his way back out to his car. A ship's horn blew mournfully over the wide glittering river.

He drove back to Bennybank slowly and went into the empty house. It wouldn't do any harm to ask Ann.

7

Jenna woke, thick-headed and groggy. A thin winter light trickled through the slit in the curtains. She grasped at her bedside alarm clock. Ten o'clock. In the morning. What had happened?

She remembered chatting to Donna and drinking cocoa the previous night. Then it was a blank. She must have crashed completely. Gus! What must he have thought when she didn't turn up at the restaurant. She staggered out of bed on shaking limbs. Her hair was a bird's nest and there were puffy dark circles under her eyes. It would take more than a hot shower to sort her out.

She was drinking her third cup of strong, black coffee when Donna joined her at the breakfast table. She waited while Donna piled her plate with pancakes and maple syrup.

'How are you this morning?' Donna

asked. 'You conked out last night. I had to help you to your room.'

'Feeling more alert thanks to this.' Jenna lifted her cup. She paused. 'Donna, what was in the cocoa?'

'What do you mean?' Donna sounded startled.

'I mean that I think I've taken a sleeping tablet. Did you make the drink?'

'No. Mum made it and asked me to take it to you.'

Had Lisette really had the gall to grind up a sleeping pill and put it in the cocoa?

'Jennifer, you look refreshed,' Lisette commented, gliding into her place at the table.

Donna fetched her toast and tea while Lisette's fingernails tapped a marching beat. Jenna could hardly bring herself to reply she was so furious.

Lisette raised her eyebrows. 'You look annoyed with me dear. You mustn't, you know. You needed a good rest.

Would you have taken my advice? No. Because you're stubborn like your father.'

Jenna pushed her chair back and left before she said something she later regretted. She'd missed her evening with Gus because of her stepmother and she couldn't forgive her.

She gathered her bag and coat wishing she was leaving the Lintons' house for good. At least her leg had improved overnight. She could put her weight on it. It was tender but not excruciating. She limped downstairs. Gus's chauffeur was there at the front of the house, ready to drive her to Thornley. Perhaps a day of baking would soothe her and restore her mood.

* * *

The stone entrance pillars and old gatehouse seemed already like old friends. Her heart beat a little faster, wanting her first view of Thornley. There it was. The great square looked

133

softer this time, glowing against the backdrop of leaden sky and sodden grass. She realised what it was. The windows were no longer black and empty. They were lit on the ground floor, cosy amber and inviting.

Gus was there on the doorstep to welcome her. His face was splattered with tiny freckles of white paint. Behind him she could hear the bang and clatter of furniture moving and a shout of alarm. Gus appeared hesitant and watchful as she greeted him, then she hugged him and his arms closed round her. Jenna felt safe immediately in his strong embrace. A prickle of awareness at his nearness made her shiver.

'Are you cold? Let's get inside.' Gus guided her in. 'How's the ankle?'

She wasn't cold. Far from it. There was a fire burning in the pit of her stomach for him. Jenna could no longer ignore it. She was extremely attracted to Gus.

'The ankle's bearing up nicely, thanks. Hey, Thornley's looking alive,' she said as they squeezed past a workman carrying a dusty bookcase.

'I've got a whole team working on it. I want the place ready for the filming of the advert at the end of the week.'

They went downstairs to the kitchens. Jenna shrieked in joy. The transformation was amazing. The ancient cooker and grubby kitchen units were gone, replaced by a gleaming, modern layout of burnished steel and polished walnut. Her pans and mixing bowls were waiting for her. A crisp, white apron hung over the back of a chair. Jenna rubbed her hands together in glee.

'I want to get started right away,' she cried.

'Wait,' Gus said.

She turned to look at him. His brown eyes were guarded and questioning.

'Where did you get to last night?'

'I'm so sorry. I, ah, fell asleep . . . ' It was lame but Jenna couldn't bring herself to tell him that Lisette had stopped her by drugging her drink. Her stepmother may have done it for her own good, for her health, but Jenna wasn't sure. She wanted it to be so. The alternative, that Lisette wanted to prevent her seeing Gus, was too shocking.

'I'm the one who should apologise,' Gus said. 'What was I thinking of, inviting you out when you were in such pain.'

'I wanted to see you last night,' she said plainly.

'Me too.' Gus's voice was hoarse. His eyes were dark liquid as he gazed at her. He put out his arms to her. 'Jenna . . . '

There was a raucous crash and they jumped apart as a chunk of ceiling plaster fell to the floor between them. Upstairs men's voices were raised in argument and there was a heavy thumping and the screech of old floorboards tested to their limit.

'Excuse me,' Gus muttered and leapt up the stairs two at a time.

Jenna's heart pounded fast. What had just happened? She didn't care about the plasterwork. Was Gus going to kiss her? Did she want him to? Would she have kissed him back? Bewildered, she did what she always did in times of crisis. She began to bake.

She opened the nearest cupboard and discovered it was full of essential ingredients. The next one held weighing scales. Gus had put a lot of care and attention into making Thornley's new kitchen perfect. Soon she was engrossed in mixing batter and thinking ahead to icing and which of the forty odd nozzles she would use to decorate the cupcakes and delicacies.

'What I don't understand is why you sent Shelley instead,' Gus said, emerging beside her from the side door of the kitchen. His hair was now liberally dusted with plaster.

'Shelley? What do you mean?' Jenna said, wooden spoon hovering over the bowl.

'Shelley was waiting for me in the restaurant. She told me you couldn't make it and that you didn't want to let me down so she came instead.'

Of all the sneaky . . . She had to hand it to Shelley. She didn't miss an opportunity.

'You seriously think I sent Shelley in my place?'

'Didn't you?'

'No, I didn't. Why should it bother you in any case? She's a beautiful girl. She evidently likes you very much. Why don't you go right ahead and date her?' Jenna couldn't help it, she sounded sharp.

'She's very attractive,' Gus agreed, making her beat the batter harder, 'but I had no wish for the dinner to be anything more than two friends meeting.'

Jenna felt immensely better hearing that but perversely she retorted, 'That's where you're going wrong. You've been alone for five years. Surely Leila would want you to find someone else and move on.'

Now it was Gus's turn to be curt. 'Leave Leila out of this. You have no idea what she would and wouldn't want. You didn't know her.'

His words stung her.

'I didn't know Leila but if she loved you she'd want you to find happiness again. If you find Shelley so darned attractive then you should ask her out properly and stop denying it!' Jenna was shouting now. She slammed down the spoon and faced him squarely.

'I don't want her, you little idiot,' Gus growled. He pulled her into his arms and suddenly his mouth was hard upon hers. Even as their lips met his softened, teasing hers apart for a deep, searching kiss.

Jenna's heartbeat quickened as she felt his body hard against hers. She cradled his head, pulling him even closer to her and wanting the kiss to last forever. Her limbs were weak with desire, a molten heat rising in her body. Gus groaned, drawing away for a ragged breath. Greedily, needing him, she pulled him back to initiate another searing kiss. Finally they paused, staring at each other.

Gus opened his mouth to speak. Gently, Jenna pressed a finger to his mouth.

'Shhh, if you're going to apologise, please don't.'

'I can't offer you anything,' Gus blurted. 'It was a mistake. We shouldn't have . . . '

Jenna's elastic heart, at first so warm and pumping with desire, now snapped back coldly and painfully into her chest. She stepped slowly from Gus who still had his arms wrapped loosely round her.

'You're right. It didn't mean anything,' she said numbly. She turned away so he couldn't see the hurt in her eyes. When she turned back, they were masked and neutral. She'd learned from Gus then. How to hide emotion and put a face on to the world.

'I'm not ready for a relationship,' Gus tried to explain.

'It was only a kiss,' Jenna said lightly. But it wasn't. She realised now how very attracted to Gus she was. It was physical agony to be standing so close to him and yet to be emotionally torn apart by his words. Oh, to be able to lean towards him and press her mouth passionately to his.

'I wish . . . ' Gus said, but didn't finish. She didn't find out what it was he wished for because a couple of burly workmen arrived complaining about woodworm in the attic and, with an apologetic smile, Gus vanished upstairs with them.

Jenna pushed the bowl from her in exasperation. Baking held no appeal. Her lips tingled from where Gus's mouth had pressed against them. She touched them wonderingly. She'd kissed Gus. She wanted him. And he wanted her too, however much he tried to run away from it.

★ ★ ★

The chauffeur drove her home late that afternoon. Jenna lay with her head back

141

on the head rest gladly. She was tired but her mind was still racing. She hadn't seen Gus again but had heard him calling to his team of workers somewhere in the depths of the house. What would they have said to one another anyway? Gus had told her he wasn't ready for a relationship. She wasn't about to argue with him, it was too humiliating. Then there was William. She would have to write to him. It was the honest thing to do. Whether Gus wanted to be together with her or not, she knew she was deeply attracted to him.

Her feelings for William were but a pale shade besides the strong emotions she felt for Gus. She'd always known she wasn't 'in love' with William but had firmly believed that love, in time, would grow between them. Now her theory of love had exploded into tiny pieces. It wasn't a logical, neat progression from friends to lovers. No, it was a violent impact that threw one sideways when least expected. Gus's kiss had made her body ache as though with a fever. She ached now, wanting him to be with her, to touch her again. Jenna banged her head back against the car seat in frustration. The chauffeur looked at her in the mirror and she closed her eyes.

★   ★   ★

Lisette was lying on a sports mat in the living-room while her physiotherapist worked her legs, gently flexing them at the knee and coaxing her patient to co-operate.

'That's all for today, Mrs Linton,' the woman said brightly and helped Lisette back into the chair. 'I'll be back tomorrow.'

'If you wish,' Lisette said curtly. 'There is not any point but,' she gave a Gallic shrug, 'no doubt you will be here.'

The woman laughed. 'It's my job to keep you fit and flexible so I'll be here.'

Jenna, who had arrived home as the

physiotherapy session was ending, politely took her to the door and showed her out. Despite her anger at Lisette, she couldn't help feeling sorry for her. Her stepmother's face was grey and hollowed today.

'Can I bring you a cup of tea?' she asked.

Lisette looked surprised to see her there. She'd been lost in her musings, none of them pleasant it would appear.

'Yes please, Jennifer. A cup of tea. Perhaps even a pot to share, no?'

Jenna smiled. It was as if a tiny crack had appeared in her stepmother's armour towards her. 'One large pot, coming up.'

Shelley was in the kitchen, eating chocolate biscuits from a pink ceramic jar.

'Oh, you're back. How was precious Thornley? Was Gus there? Did he tell you about our date last night?'

Jenna gritted her teeth. She said nothing and concentrated on boiling the kettle and finding the teabags. But

Shelley wouldn't let it go.

'You won't get him you know. I don't understand how you've managed to ensnare him this far . . . but it won't last. You've got nothing to offer a man like Gus. But I do. I've got the looks, the charm and I'm in it for the long run. Wait and see.'

Shelley had no idea. Jenna wasn't even in the running. Gus didn't want to be with her even as his body reacted to hers.

'I'm leaving,' she heard herself say. She didn't know where she would go but she couldn't stand to be in the same house as Shelley any longer. Perhaps she could beg for floor space with Ann's cousin Lesley. Or she could rent somewhere cheap now she was being paid by Gus.

'Leaving Glasgow?' Shelley asked, not bothering to hide her gloating. *I've won*, it cried out.

'No, I've a job to do here. I'll find another place to live.'

Jenna took the tray of tea and a plate

of biscuits through to Lisette. Shelley trailed behind her. *Let her be disappointed*, Jenna thought savagely. She refused to be chased from the city. She'd go in her own sweet time.

'Jenna's moving out,' Shelley announced to her mother.

Jenna expected Lisette to be cheered by this. After all, she was a reluctant hostess. So she was unprepared for Lisette's dismay. Quickly she removed the tea cup from her stepmother's trembling grasp and set it safely beside her on the small occasional table.

'*Non, non.* You must not go. Norman would not want it.' The old woman shook her head in agitation.

'But Mummy, Jenna wants to go. She hates it here. Besides, I'd like to turn that spare room into a little sewing study for you. What do you think? We could be so cosy there in the evenings. You can show me how to embroider, like you wanted to last winter. I'd like to learn.' Shelley's voice was low and softly persuasive. There was a strong thread of confidence too. She was able to wind her mother round her little finger usually.

'I won't hear of it Jennifer,' Lisette said. 'You must stay, for Norman's sake.'

Shelley looked shocked. 'Mummy . . . ' she began.

Lisette waved her hand in angry dismissal. 'On this matter I will not be budged. Jennifer, I will hear no more of leaving, *n'est-ce pas?*'

Jenna could've felt resentment at Lisette's peremptory order but she intuited that behind her sharp manner, Lisette was truly distressed at her suggestion of leaving.

'I won't leave,' she promised, earning herself a dagger look from Shelley. She couldn't please both of them.

She left them there and went upstairs to write to William.

Her pen hesitated over the blank paper. What to say? After all, he'd dumped her when she needed him most.

She hadn't acknowledged this at the time. She'd made excuses for him and hoped they could reconnect. With fresh eyes she saw now that she was no use to him without a job and an income. That hurt.

He'd hinted recently that he'd come to visit her but only once he'd heard from Ann that she was working again. She wondered if he'd loved her at all. Whatever his motivations, she owed him a letter of explanation. She hoped he would understand. They could still be friends. She chewed the top of the pen.

Dear William . . .

* * *

Gus was in pain. It wasn't bodily but it might as well have been. It had taken all his strength that day not to rush back to the kitchen and sweep Jenna up in his arms and kiss her passionately until she melted against him. There was a soreness right there in the middle of his chest. A throbbing ache. A longing for her.

He had kissed her first in anger which had turned rapidly to desire. But then he'd told her it was a mistake and that he wasn't ready for a relationship. Gus groaned. He was an idiot!

He was lonely and had been for a very long time. Now he'd found someone he liked, a lot. It wouldn't hurt to enjoy himself a little. To alleviate the dreadful isolation which wrapped itself lover-like around him in any company.

With Jenna he didn't feel alone. It wasn't love of course. He loved only Leila. But it was something good. Gus rose slowly from his study chair at Bennybank where he'd been sitting staring at his computer trying to sort out his accounts. He left the screen bright with the wallpaper of Leila's laughing face to the camera. He put on his thick winter coat and whistled for Scout. There was a place that he had to go. Now.

8

It was pitch black outside and the snow had started falling again. Wispy white flakes floated down like little stars tumbling from the sky. They melted on impact leaving a jewel of water in their place, on Gus's head and shoulders and on Scout's wiry fur. Christmas trees had appeared as if by magic in all the windows, wound round with twinkling coloured fairy lights. Their pretty colours cheered him momentarily until he was reminded that another lonely Christmas Day beckoned.

The churchyard gates were shut and for a moment he dreaded they were locked but they swung open readily at his touch. He was unafraid, standing there at the entrance to the cemetery in the darkness. The outline of the old church was comforting, like a squat and reassuring gate keeper.

Someone, the minister perhaps, had placed electric candles behind the tiny paned windows to the left of the wooden chapel door. The white lights shone as little circular beacons, winking as the power to them fluctuated. Scout gave a soft woof.

'Yes, old chap, we're going in. Now no chasing the wildlife tonight.'

He let the dog off the lead.

The grass rustled like old silk as his feet found the familiar trail along the soft dampness of the path to the headstones. The angel stood in vigil, her outline almost lost in the night. Above, Gus's view of the heavens was fringed with the branches and wisped twigs of the winter birches.

'It's me,' he said unnecessarily. A little breeze stirred up, making the winter browned grasses whisper. 'I need to talk.' He paused and gave a self-conscious chuckle. 'It's a funny time to do so, I know, but some things can't wait.'

Scout plunged from the undergrowth

after some small dark blur of a mammal. Gus's heart jumped twitchily.

'Maybe I'm foolish coming here so late,' he said, 'but I wanted to tell you . . . I've found someone. Not like Kate,' he added swiftly, then stopped. 'At least I very much hope not.' He thought again of his conversation with Ann.

★　★　★

In the end he'd dropped by at Lesley's flat on his way to Thornley early that morning, still hearing the echo of Shelley's throwaway remark. He felt oddly guilty at doing so. He knew Jenna, didn't he? He shouldn't be sneaking around behind her back asking about her. But Kate had wounded him more than he thought. She'd shaken his belief in his own judgement about people. Could he trust Jenna? He wanted to badly but he still found himself there in the west end outside the smart stone tenement, looking up at the fourth floor window.

He was half expecting no-one to answer at that hour of the morning. But the buzzer rang letting him in through the communal close door. Ann peered down at him from the first floor landing.

'Hey!' She welcomed him in. 'Are you looking for Lesley? She's not here, I'm afraid.'

'Actually I was hoping for a quick word with you,' Gus said. He followed her graceful skip up the stone stairwell and into an immaculate home of polished wooden floors, cream living-room suite and the scent of sandalwood and lavender.

'What can I do for you?' Ann asked curiously. He saw she was working. A row of beautiful embroidered dresses hung from a rack in the centre of the room. A thick workbook lay open showing columns of figures while a laptop lay beside it charging. Ann closed the book over. 'I'm working crazy hours right now,' she said with a grin, 'so I'm glad of a break. Coffee?'

He nodded. He didn't want coffee but it was good to have a moment to collect himself. He let her slam about cheerfully in Lesley's kitchen to arrive back with two mismatched glazed pottery mugs full to the brim with a strong, aromatic brew.

'Thanks.' He took it and sipped, wondering how to begin.

Ann saved him by starting first.

'Is this about Jenna? Is she alright?'

'Yes, at least I hope so. She was meant to meet me last night for dinner but couldn't make it.' He thought of Shelley's attempt at seduction and her scornful words. 'I'll see her this morning at Thornley. She's baking there today.'

Suddenly talking about her made him feel disloyal to even contemplate asking her best friend what he wanted to know. Shouldn't he take Jenna on merit? He liked her very much. He was attracted to her for certain. Nothing she'd done suggested a hidden agenda.

But yet, there was a worm of caution in his stomach. Kate's behaviour had damaged him. Gus rubbed his face wearily.

'Gus? Is everything OK?' Ann asked kindly.

'Jenna's friend William, what's he like?' Gus said in a rush. He couldn't ask about Jenna, he just couldn't. But he could enquire about William.

There was a hesitant silence. Ann pulled the charger on her laptop and threw it accurately into the laptop case. 'William,' she said heavily. 'Why do you ask?'

'Sorry.' Gus stood abruptly. 'I should go.'

'No, no, it's OK.' Ann stood too. 'William's got a few problems to work through. He's employed by me since he lost all his income. I . . . '

'That's all I need to know, thanks Ann,' Gus interrupted. He left quickly, embarrassed by his own actions, leaving a surprised Ann watching him from the tenement window.

So Shelley was right. William had lost all his money. The question was, how? Shelley's angry words rang in his head. *She's not the sweet little girl you think she is. She's a gold digger like Kate. She wiped out her boyfriend's money.*

He didn't want to think about it any more. It left a sourness in his mouth. Instead, he'd rushed back to his car, already thinking about the day ahead of him at Thornley and another chance to be with Jenna.

★　★　★

Gus twisted his wedding ring now on his finger. 'I've found someone I like,' he repeated. 'She's a friend and could be something more. She can't replace you Leila. No-one can. I'm not in love with Jenna,' he paused, conjuring up her delicate features, her eyes huge in a face still too thin, framed by her dark hair with its natural coppery highlights. A flicker of pleasure stirred inside him as he thought of her. He longed to stroke her hair and to bend his head to let their lips join. More than that, he wanted to hear her laugh and chat with him. He wanted to know her secrets, her fears and her ambitions. He wanted to know Jenna as well as he knew himself.

'You'd like her, Leila,' he said to the damp, night air. 'I know you would. I could see the two of you getting along like a house on fire.'

Scout reappeared at his feet with a sneezy sigh and sat heavily. Gus felt the little dog's wet body soak warmly into his trouser leg. It was time to go but he was reluctant to leave. The black night was a place where he could think without distraction, a place to be honest with himself.

'I ran away from Jenna,' he admitted. Scout grunted, thinking Gus was talking to him. He wagged his stumpy tail lovingly.

'I told her I wasn't ready for a relationship. I pushed her away.' Gus groaned. 'What madness. I was scared.

I'm still scared. What if it doesn't work out?' He kicked at an old tuft of grass heads beside the path, making Scout stand to attention, ears pricked for prey. 'Where's my courage? Give it to me Leila. Let me at least try . . . '

A night owl flew on silent wings over them. Gus saw it briefly before it topped the birches and disappeared. He whistled low for Scout and together they took the path back to the gates. Gus was at peace. Tomorrow he would speak to Jenna.

★ ★ ★

'It should look like breadcrumbs.'

'Like this?' Donna asked uncertainly. She offered the mixing bowl to Jenna.

'That's it, great. The trick is to make sure the butter is really cold and then slice it into the flour. If you overwork it, the pastry will be too greasy.'

Donna, flushed with success and under Jenna's instruction, trickled a little water into the bowl to make the finished dough. 'Thanks for bringing me today. This is just what I needed.'

Jenna nodded in sympathy. There had been yet another argument between Lisette and Donna that morning over Stewart, leaving an atmosphere thick with tension. Jenna had been glad to pull on her coat and wait for the chauffeur. On the spur of the moment she'd asked Donna to come with her. Now she was glad she'd done so; her stepsister looked so happy and relaxed for once.

'This is a wonderful old house,' Donna commented as she rolled out the dough.

The sweet scents of sugar and almonds rose in the warmth of the kitchen. The windows were misted by their baking and from upstairs came the sound of Christmas carols. Mrs Russell was in, taking charge of the last of the clearing up now that the work teams had finished renovating the ground floor. Today they would begin refreshing the bedrooms.

Jenna thought of Gus. Would she see him today? Surely he'd want to meet with his workers and tell them what he wanted upstairs? In any case, she couldn't avoid him forever. She would play it cool, she decided. She'd pretend that nothing had happened between them, if that made it easier for Gus.

Her heart squeezed painfully as she instructed herself. It was ridiculous! Even thinking about seeing him made her body react. It wouldn't do. She took a few deep breaths and forced herself to concentrate on the baking sheet in front of her. Donna gave her a hesitant smile. Jenna realised she was waiting for some sort of response.

'Sorry, Donna, I was miles away,' she said. 'Yes, Thornley is rather lovely. Even before the renovations it had such a welcoming feel to it.'

'Is Gus going to be here today? It would be nice to catch up,' Donna said shyly.

There went Jenna's heart again, thumping loudly in her chest so she was sure Donna could hear it too. How was she to play it cool when her body betrayed her so readily?

'I don't know. Right, are you ready to pop those in the top oven?' She changed the subject abruptly.

Surprised, Donna handed over the baking sheet with its circles of hopeful pastry. They were uneven in thickness and size but Jenna didn't have the heart to tell her. They were a first attempt and at least a few would be edible. The point was more to distract Donna from her emotional woes. Besides, she realised she was enjoying her stepsister's company. Donna was the quiet one, getting along with things without much fuss. It was pleasant to work alongside her, knowing there'd be no outbursts or storming off. She couldn't see how Shelley would work like this.

'Why did you start writing to me?' Jenna asked impulsively.

Donna blushed and brushed her fringe forward as if to hide under its thick dark layer. 'It was just after you'd

161

visited us on your way to France.'

'That's right. I stayed a couple of nights before I went to the airport. When I got back from the continent and got home, there was a letter from you waiting on the mat. It was a really nice surprise in amongst the bills,' Jenna grinned, 'but totally unexpected.'

'Your visit was like a breath of fresh air,' Donna said slowly. 'Even then I was in love with Stewart but couldn't see a way forward. You were . . . you were so bright and confident, so beautiful. You knew where you were going in life. I suppose I wanted to somehow be a part of it. Like it would rub off on me.' She halted, self-consciously, daring a peek at Jenna.

Jenna was astonished. Was that honestly how Donna had seen her? It was as if she was talking about someone completely different. For a moment she didn't recognise herself in that description. Beautiful and confident? She took herself back in time and tried to remember the old Jenna. Her business at that time had been growing. So much so that she'd had trouble keeping up with demand. She loved it. The trip to France had included a patisserie course under a well-known French sous-chef. Her health had been perfect and she was so happy with life. Then it had all come crashing down upon her.

She didn't speak, not wanting to break the spell that was allowing Donna to talk so openly. Instead she nodded encouragingly. It worked. Donna went on.

'It wasn't all about me though. I remember feeling guilty that we'd grown up together but we never got to know each other. Not truly. I know you felt that too. It's partly the reason why you came to stay that year, isn't it? It felt like an opportunity. If I wrote to you regularly and you wrote back, we could become friends.'

'Oh, Donna, we are friends.' Jenna put her arms around her and hugged her tight. After a second, Donna was hugging her back. When they stepped apart, both tearful, it was to find they had spread flour marks liberally over each other.

Donna laughed first. Jenna had never heard her laugh with so much joy and exuberance. She had a snorting, infectious giggle which made Jenna join in. When she had control of herself again, Jenna knew she had a bond with Donna and was determined never to let it wane.

The shrill bleep of the oven cooker sounded and they both ran to see the results of Donna's baking.

'Not bad for a first attempt,' Jenna encouraged.

Donna stared in dismay at the lumpy little cakes.

'No, really,' Jenna said gamely.

Then there was a snort and Donna was off again with an infectious giggle that just wouldn't stop.

When they had calmed and sat with a cup of tea in the kitchen, Jenna had an idea.

'How about helping me out? I'm

never going to produce the quantities I need for Gus's Christmas competition.'

'Do you mean that? I'm not terribly good at baking, am I?'

'You've only just begun. You might not believe it but I think with a bit of training you could do well. What do you say?'

Donna's reply was to give her a crushing hug, heartfelt.

'That's a yes then,' Jenna said breathlessly.

* * *

There was a winding path which led from the back door of Thornley House, through the vegetable garden, along between the back lawns and up into a wooded copse on a small hillock. In the early afternoon, Jenna found herself following the stone cobbles, relishing the biting winter wind which stung her cheeks and whipped her hair around her face. Her ankle was almost healed. She could press her foot to the ground with only a very slight discomfort.

There had been no sign of Gus and she had roller-coasted from relief to disappointment to annoyance and back to relief. Now she wasn't sure what she felt. A brisk walk would clear her thoughts, she hoped, before she went back to work.

Taking Donna on was a positive step. She did need an assistant and perhaps it would help Donna to break free from her stifling home life and find her independence. She had given her stepsister an opportunity and it was up to her now what she did with it, but she was convinced Donna would make a go of it.

At the top of the hillock she paused to gather her breath. The view was fantastic. She stood at the edge of the woods and soaked it in.

Thornley stood magnificently alone in a swathe of brown-patched grounds. Beyond it were hedgerows, mere darkened skeletons at this time of year, and the occasional huge tree standing sentry in the middle of the fields.

In the distance she could just make out what she thought was the sea. Its grey waters merged with the silver sky. The air was icy and clean and when she sucked it into her lungs it made her teeth hurt.

She stretched out her arms to the world, feeling the muscles stretch and her bones click. She felt good and strong. She was aware that her hair had thickened and shined since moving to the city and her sinuses were clear, while her cough had disappeared. She had the strangest impulse to run or climb and to use her body while it was young and lithe and powerful.

'That's what having energy does to you,' she said to the air.

She squinted down at the house. A figure was walking along the path. It had passed the vegetable garden with its broken down stalks and empty plots. Now it was moving quickly through the russet grasses. It was Gus!

Jenna hid behind the nearest tree to

watch. Should she run? How foolish. It was only Gus. They were adults, weren't they? They could be civil to each other, they could work it out. Her pulse sped.

She edged out from the trees, embarrassed to be found hiding like a child.

Then he was there, right at her side. 'Hello Jenna.'

'Gus.' His name stuck in her dry throat. She kicked at old leaves below her shoes. When she dared look up again, he was smiling. Why did he have to have such an effect on her?

'Donna told me you'd gone for a walk. I guessed you'd come up here. When I was visiting Thornley regularly, this is where I used to like to go.'

With Leila? She couldn't bring herself to ask. There was more than a little flicker of jealousy in the question. She was suddenly appalled that she was envious of his dead wife.

Gus went on, 'You've taken on an assistant, I'm told. It's a great idea. The first lot of cakes went down extremely well with our clients Lesley tells me. We need more, lots more. And I want a big display on show at Thornley for the filming.'

So he wanted to pretend that nothing had happened between them. That it was business as usual. Fine. Two could play at that game.

'Don't worry, I won't let you down. You'll get the orders for the agency.' It came out stiff and formal. She couldn't help it. He'd spoiled everything between them, she thought angrily. The friendly easiness was gone. She couldn't forget his kiss. They couldn't go back from it to being just friends.

'I must get back,' she said. 'Donna's waiting for me.'

She went to brush past him to get to the safety of the woods and the path down. Gus caught her arm. Jenna stared up at him in surprise. His grip was strong but careful.

'I talk a lot when I'm nervous,' he said.

'And why are you nervous?' She wouldn't let him off easily.

'You know why.' He let her arm go and rubbed his face.

With a pang she saw his tired eyes. Then she steeled herself. It served him right if he'd had a sleepless night. He'd given her one. She'd lain awake re-living his embrace and his parting words over and over until she'd fallen into a deep sleep and woken unrefreshed.

'Gus . . . ' she began.

'I want to try,' he interrupted, his warm brown eyes seeking hers. 'Will you give me another chance? I was a fool to run away but I was scared. Jenna?'

Her heart sang. She reached for his hand and felt it close round hers, strong and capable, warm and reassuring. All those things and more — a connection between their flesh of pure energy, sparking between them, promising delight. Slowly and with infinite joy, she leaned up and kissed him on the lips.

He pulled her into his embrace and

kissed her deeply until they were both shaken by it.

When they drew back breathlessly, Gus said, 'You haven't answered me.'

Jenna felt a giggle rise up like bubbles in lemonade until it burst out of her and floated away into the crisp air.

'Yes, yes, yes!'

'I'd like to take things slowly,' he said. 'I'm not sure what I have to offer anyone. Can you understand that?'

'I think you underestimate yourself, but yes, I do understand. Slow is fine.' Jenna kissed him softly.

She didn't want to rush into anything either. She'd only just disentangled herself emotionally from William and even if it was a pale shadow of what she felt for Gus, still it had left a shadow of guilt. Mainly it was guilt that she had let William use her for so long as a source of funds and a place to offload his grumbles. She'd been deluded by him. With Gus, she hoped to trust again in her judgement. Her instinct told her he wouldn't let her down.

They walked through the trees and back down the path to Thornley, arms entwined.

★ ★ ★

Back in the Glasgow townhouse, Lisette had called for Shelley.

'Darling, has Gus called you to Thornley House yet?'

'Apart from the filming of the advert at the end of the week, no,' she said sullenly.

Shelley sank into an armchair and waited. There was some scheme in her mother's mind. She knew the look of concentration on the older woman's face.

'You must try harder to fascinate him,' Lisette reproached. She tapped her perfect nails, French polished, on the armrests of her wheelchair.

'I do try, Mummy,' Shelley protested. 'It's Jenna. She's got her claws into him. How, I don't know, she's nothing to look at. In fact . . . '

172

'Enough!' Lisette said sharply.

Shelley leapt out of the armchair to stalk around the room. 'It's your fault for making her stay. She wanted to leave, for goodness sake. You should've let her. That was the answer!'

Lisette shook her head. 'No, I don't want to argue with you over that again. There's a better way to, how do you say, deflect, Jennifer from our Gus. She needs to realise he is not for her, n'est-ce pas? Now, I saw a letter from a boyfriend to Jennifer. Perhaps she is homesick. A visit from this William might be a wonderful surprise.'

'You read her mail?' Shelley said admiringly.

Lisette dismissed the comment. She tapped her chin thoughtfully.

'I need you to do something for me.'

9

'What do you think?' Donna smoothed her apron down nervously.

Jenna looked appreciatively at the dining room table. It was draped with a starched white linen tablecloth edged with lace. The table was set for six with shining cutlery and crockery whose cream and gold pattern perfectly complemented the sprayed gold Christmas decorations and silver crackers. In the centre, Donna had placed a crystal bowl filled with gold-wrapped chocolates.

'I love it,' she said. 'What's your menu?'

'For starters I've made cream of asparagus soup, for main I'm attempting a traditional roast turkey and trimmings and for dessert a rich chocolate mousse,' replied Donna nervously.

'I'm impressed. I had no idea you

were a home cook.'

Donna laughed. 'I'm not. At least I wasn't until a couple of days ago. I enjoyed the baking so much that I've decided to branch out into other areas of cooking. I have a confession to make — I won't be doing this alone. Stewart loves cooking.'

Donna had invited Stewart for a meal at home that evening and asked Jenna and Gus to come too. Safety in numbers, she'd joked, telling Jenna that Lisette and Shelley would be joining them.

'So your Mum came round to the idea?' Jenna asked.

Donna lost her happy smile and sighed. 'She forbade me to invite Stewart to dinner as you know. I'm sure you heard the sharp exchanges last night.'

'It was hard to miss,' Jenna admitted wryly. She'd been reading in her room, trying to unwind from a long day baking at Thornley when the raised voices had penetrated her bedroom.

She'd been prepared to go down to defend Donna but after listening for a short while reckoned Donna was more than holding her own for once.

'The outcome was me telling her that if she didn't approve, then I was going to invite him anyway and pay for all the food myself.'

Jenna was amazed. She made a show of letting her jaw drop and exaggeratedly shutting it again. 'Wow.'

'I surprised myself,' Donna agreed. 'It was only possible due to you. The money I made as your assistant is being put to good use.'

'I'm glad, and perhaps after tonight Lisette will begin to see what a nice guy Stewart is.'

'I do hope so,' Donna said fervently, 'but if not, I won't let up. I'm going to start saving from my job. It'll take a while but eventually me and Stewart will be able to get a place of our own.'

'That's the spirit.' Jenna hugged her. 'Now, can I help with the dessert?'

'I should say no, it's all in hand but . . . yes, you can absolutely make the dessert!'

* * *

Jenna chose a softly clinging rose coloured dress to wear. As she slipped it over her head she was reminded that she'd previously worn it during that summer visit to France.

Memories came back quickly as she adjusted the side zip. It evoked the younger, confident Jenna whose life was great and whose ambitions knew no end. The world was hers for the taking. Since then she hadn't worn it. She'd lost too much weight for it to sit nicely on her and her colour was too wan for it to be pretty. With satisfaction she saw that her curves had returned. She had a waist and womanly hips again.

Would Gus think her attractive? She pushed tiny rose earrings into her ear lobes and brushed her hair until it shone. There was no need for make-up, she had a glow to her skin that was enough.

She was a little late entering the dining room and so was the last person there. There was a chill to the air that had nothing to do with the central heating. Lisette sat at the head of the table. Her face was white and her expression icy. Shelley sat at the other end, making no effort to chat. Her face was sulkily bored as if she had been forced to attend and wanted to make that quite evident.

Gus sat to Shelley's left, opposite Stewart. He was making polite conversation, asking Stewart about his work. He was the only one who looked at ease and his welcoming smile to Jenna made her melt in the middle.

Stewart's round features were stiff with unease despite Gus's friendly chat. Jenna wondered if Donna had told him about her mother's reaction to the meal.

Donna herself sat beside Stewart with a smile firmly in place but Jenna could see panic rising in her eyes. In front of each of them was a small bowl of soup. The aroma was delicious but no-one was eating.

'Sorry I'm late, Donna,' she said lightly, taking her place beside Gus and earning a frown from Shelley. 'I know it's rude but I'm ravenous so would you mind if we started on this lovely soup? It smells wonderful.'

Donna threw her a grateful look. 'Please tuck in. There's warmed bread too. I'll get it.'

'You begin your starter,' Stewart said, placing his hand proprietorially on hers. 'I'll get the bread. After all, you're in charge of the main course.'

'Which smells great,' Gus joined in, and the conversation began to move and become more relaxed in spite of Lisette's silent presence.

Jenna noticed she'd hardly touched her soup before they had all finished and the plates were whisked away by Stewart. Soon even Shelley had been persuaded by Gus to converse. He flattered her unashamedly, so much so that Shelley flicked little snide glances at Jenna as if to say, *he's mine after all*.

She ignored them. The cosy pressure of Gus's leg against hers under the table was reassurance, a little communication between them and a reminder of their promise to each other to take things slowly but surely.

'Are you remembering the wedding shoot is tomorrow?' Gus said to Shelley.

'I can't wait,' Shelley told him. 'I'm going to make the perfect bride for you Gus. You will not be disappointed.'

Gus laughed. 'Great. I'm not the bridegroom though. Lesley's booked an actor for that role. I want to make the advert as professional as possible.'

'Oh, you'd make a great groom,' Shelley purred.

'That reminds me,' Gus turned to the rest of them. 'Quite a number of my agency clients will be there tomorrow; it's going to be a little pre-Christmas party. Donna I know you're going to be helping Jenna with the catering, so

Stewart, will you come? Lisette?'

Stewart immediately agreed. Jenna got the impression that he'd follow Donna into flames if it was needed. He was clearly besotted by her.

Lisette nodded. She had eaten nothing of her main course. Donna looked upset.

'Is there something wrong, Mum? Is it not cooked properly?'

'I'm not hungry.'

Donna took her mother's plate unhappily. Jenna tried not to be angry with Lisette. It was as if she was deliberately trying to sabotage Donna's dinner party. Wasn't it enough that poor Donna had had to pay for the whole meal? Anyone could see the love between Donna and Stewart. It would take more than her family's disapproval to break them up.

'Who'll pull a cracker with me?' Jenna suggested, trying to lift the mood.

'Yeah, why not,' Shelley said. She reached over and grasped the paper end with its firecracker taper.

Jenna pulled and the cracker sparked with a loud bang. Shelley came away with the cracker. Her look of triumph was almost comical. Did she honestly have to beat Jenna at everything? Why was it all a competition?

'Well done . . . now put on your party hat,' she said jokingly.

Shelley took the hat and flung it at her. 'It's more your style.' The fool's hat landed on Jenna's plate.

'Let me take that,' Stewart said hurriedly, his kind, round face flustered. He removed the plate along with other used crockery to the kitchen.

Donna brought in the desserts at that point and placed a demitasse of dark chocolate mousse in front of each of them. Lisette pushed hers away.

'I don't feel very good . . . ' Her face was blanched of any colour and without warning she slumped sideways in her chair and was horribly still.

'Mum!' Donna cried in horror.

Gus was already out of his chair and calling for an ambulance on his mobile phone. Shelley sat frozen in her chair.

Stewart shouted, 'I'll get a blanket,' and ran out of the room.

Jenna went quickly to her stepmother's side. She felt for a pulse and was relieved to find one, faint and thready but there. A tiny trickle of saliva dribbled from the corner of Lisette's mouth. Jenna took a napkin and dabbed her chin.

Please, oh please, let it not be a stroke, Jenna prayed. She and Lisette hadn't seen eye to eye since she arrived at the Lintons' but suddenly Jenna wished for more time to get to know her. She needed to find a way through to her. It would be too cruel if Lisette succumbed to illness.

The ambulance arrived swiftly and two green-suited paramedics armed with medical kits took over the dining room. They looked incongruous amongst the remains of Donna's beautiful meal. The china was scattered and smeared with the food, the silver crackers lay there untouched except for Jenna's and the delicate cups of dessert were ignored in the frenzy of activity surrounding Lisette.

Donna was sobbing with Stewart's comforting arms around her. Shelley had disappeared but Jenna could hear her moving about upstairs. Perhaps she was preparing her mother's bedroom in the event she didn't have to go to hospital, Jenna thought.

Gus was talking to the paramedics, explaining what had happened. Lisette lay on a stretcher while one of the paramedics kneeled over her. Her flaccid cheeks were cut into by the elastic of an oxygen mask. She looked so defenceless and old that Jenna wanted to cry. Instead, when the paramedic moved back to speak into his walkie talkie, she moved forward and knelt to hold Lisette's hand. The old woman's eyelids flickered.

'She's coming round,' Jenna said a few moments later.

Lisette opened her eyes and the paramedic gently pushed Jenna out of the way and took her place. He checked her signs again until he seemed satisfied. Then he asked questions and wanted a nod or shake of the head for answers. After what felt like a long time, he stood up.

'We're going to move your mother out to the ambulance.'

'Are you taking her to hospital?' Donna asked. Her tears had dried and she was quietly controlled.

The man lifted his shoulders. 'Maybe.'

'I'm coming with you,' Donna said.

The paramedic, a large burly man, looked as if he was going to say no, but instead he turned back to his patient to speak gently to her. With a nod to his colleague, they lifted the stretcher. Donna followed them.

Gus came immediately to Jenna and hugged her.

'She'll be fine. She's in good hands.'

Jenna leaned in against him, needing his strength.

'Oh Gus, what if she isn't OK? I feel terrible about it. I . . . I thought she was withdrawn tonight to indicate her disapproval of the meal. Instead she was suffering without telling us.'

Gus kissed her lips gently. 'She's a complicated lady. It's not your fault. Now we have to hope that she's recovering and focus on looking after her.'

'Yes, yes, you're right. I'll go and help Shelley make up her bed for when she needs it.'

She had to be doing something. The waiting was agony. Gus must have realised this because he nodded. Before he let her go, he kissed her sweetly.

At that moment and with that tender gesture, something clicked inside her. She was in love with Gus. He wasn't just the most physically appealing man she'd ever met. It wasn't simply that she desired him with a heat that bordered on feverish. His personality and his caring nature were just as important to her. She loved him!

Jenna half-ran for the stairs, her mind in turmoil. There was no way she could tell him. Hadn't they agreed to take things slowly? Gus had told her he wasn't sure of what he could offer her. He'd made no sweeping promises. He certainly hadn't mentioned love. To him, they were two friends who were also slightly more, sharing kisses and caresses and a degree of intimacy. But they weren't lovers. Not two people in love.

Making Lisette's bedroom ready for her would take her mind off her quandary. Jenna pushed open the door expecting to find Shelley there but the room was empty. It was neat and tidy and sparsely furnished to allow room for the wheelchair. There was a specially installed elevator in the house so that Lisette could get upstairs.

Donna had told Jenna how her mother refused to have a bedroom on the ground floor. There was a delicate fragrance of lavender in the room and she saw a vase full of the pale purple sprigs on the windowsill. She wondered if Lisette was reminded of France when she smelt them.

On the bedside cabinet was a photo frame. Jenna picked it up. It was a picture of her father and Lisette sitting on a stone wall, the French countryside behind them. They were laughing to the photographer as they sat close together, holding hands. She put it down carefully. There was such an open look of happiness on Norman's face. She recognised that look now. He was clearly a man in love.

'How dare you. What are you doing in here?'

Jenna spun round to see Shelley marching towards her, her brows drawn.

'I was going to help you prepare your mother's room. Where were you?' she challenged.

Shelley looked taken aback. She'd obviously assumed that Jenna would wilt under her question. 'I . . . I was . . . '

'Look, it doesn't matter where you were,' Jenna interrupted, not wanting to have an argument. 'Let's turn down the bed and get a hot water bottle and maybe an extra duvet.'

Shelley stood there mulishly. She wasn't taking orders from Jenna, her stance said.

'Suit yourself.' Jenna brushed past her, suddenly impatient. Lisette was the most important consideration right now, not Shelley's emotions.

However, Shelley did follow her downstairs and took the heated water bottle when it was ready.

They had the room sorted when they heard the paramedics talking. Donna burst in, looking somewhat relieved. 'They're not taking her to hospital. They're bringing her upstairs now. She's alright. It's a viral infection that's taking its toll.'

'Are they sure?' Shelley asked sharply.

Donna shrugged. 'They're the experts. Besides, Mum refused to go to hospital. She's told them she'll be perfectly fine here.' She ignored her sister's derisory sniff and busied herself by organising the bed despite the fact that it was ready.

Jenna made no comment. Donna needed to be active. Then the paramedics were lifting Lisette competently onto her bed. Soon they were gone with strict instructions to phone without delay if her condition changed in any way. However, the burly man reassured them, it was a virus which she was fighting off. She needed plenty of fluids and bed rest. Some viruses could be nasty, he went on, and it would be best if someone stayed with her during the night just to be certain she didn't take a turn for the worse.

'I'll sit up with her,' Donna said.

'I'm not going to argue with that,' Shelley said. 'If it's only a cold then there's no real worry. Besides, I need my beauty sleep for tomorrow's shoot.'

'I'll help you prepare,' Jenna told Donna. 'You'll need a jug of water and cups. I'll make you up a flask of coffee too; it's going to be a long night.'

Gus found her in the kitchen as she waited for the kettle to boil. Again, that lift of her heart, that thrill at his nearness overwhelmed her. *I love you,* she wanted to say. Instead she smiled to reassure him all was well.

'I hope Lisette hasn't made a mistake insisting on staying home,' Gus said. 'Will you and Donna manage by yourselves tonight? Do you want me to stay?'

She wanted him to stay, with her tonight and forever. Jenna bit back the words and shook her head. 'We'll be OK. You should go home, Gus.'

'Call me if you need me. Promise? Any time, day or night. I'll come as soon as I can.'

'Thank you.' She yearned to hold him tightly, to keep him there with her. But he wasn't hers, not deeply and truly hers. She wished it could be different. Still, Gus was promising her trust and steadfastness and those were things she needed right now too. She couldn't imagine William offering her support so quickly. He was more likely to moan that his situation was worse than

Lisette's. How she could ever have been taken in by him? It was as if a veil had been lifted from her eyes where William was concerned.

When Gus had gone, she took the flask and water upstairs to Donna. She was sitting on an upright wooden chair beside her mother's bed.

Lisette looked small and vulnerable under the duvet. Only her grey hair was visible, mussed and tufted. It brought home how ill she was feeling. Lisette was always so beautifully turned out.

'OK?' Jenna whispered.

Donna nodded, trying to smile. 'Go to bed, Jenna.'

She fell asleep instantly and dreamlessly, only to be woken what seemed like minutes later by being shaken and someone calling her name. Disorientated, she sat up, rubbing her eyes. Donna stood there, her face panicked.

'It's Mum. She's so hot and sweaty and she's mumbling. I can't make out what she's saying. Should I call the hospital?'

Jenna followed her to Lisette's bedroom, now awake with an icy fear. The room smelt sour and airless. In the bed, Lisette tossed restlessly, muttering. Jenna put a hand on her forehead. It was soaking wet and very hot. Her stepmother stared at her.

'It's alright,' Jenna soothed. 'We're going to cool you down.' She turned to go and get flannels and cold water. Lisette gripped her arm with a surprising strength.

'Norman's little girl. Where are you Norman? Why aren't you listening? Norman?'

She was rambling and delirious. Jenna gently disentangled her hand and ran to get the flannels.

When she got back to the bedroom it was to see Donna swaying from fatigue.

'Go to bed,' she ordered, repeating what Donna had said to her earlier.

'No, no, I can't,' Donna said. 'I can't leave her.' She sat heavily on the chair as if her legs would no longer support her.

'You're no use to anyone if you're exhausted,' Jenna said. 'You must rest. I'll take over now and in the morning it'll be your turn again.'

That did the trick. Donna nodded, clearly seeing the sense in what she was saying. She stumbled to the door and away.

Jenna rinsed the first flannel in water that she'd dropped ice cubes into, and laid it carefully on her stepmother's forehead. Lisette gave a little moan. The flannel was burning hot within seconds. Jenna repeated the process with a second flannel. It too was quickly heated by Lisette's feverish skin. She wondered whether she should phone for help. The third flannel took longer though. With a sigh of relief, Jenna continued her cooling. Lisette mumbled and called out. Jenna heard her own name and her father's in amongst some she didn't recognise.

Lisette grabbed her. The flannel slid from her head. She sat up, gaunt and with bloodshot eyes.

'He wasn't moving, you see. That's how I knew. He had left me all alone. I was angry at him for doing so. I thought, how will I survive? I was thinking of his selfishness. If he hadn't insisted on driving home that day, this wouldn't have happened. He was always such a stubborn man.'

With a chill, Jenna realised Lisette was talking about the day of the accident that had claimed her father's life.

'I blamed him terribly,' Lisette cried, a ragged sob escaping her. She fell back onto the soaked pillows, turning this way and that as the fever harried her.

Jenna laid a fresh cold compress on her forehead, willing her to get better. If she didn't show some sign of improvement within the half hour, she was determined to phone for medical help. After a minute or so, Lisette sighed and murmured. She opened her eyes and looked straight at Jenna. Her gaze was lucid. 'Jennifer, you remind me so of him. I see you every day and it brings me a memory of Norman.'

'Do you still blame him?' Jenna dared to ask. She was fearful of bringing on the fever again but she needed to know.

'No, not any more,' the older woman said. 'I hated him for leaving me. Let us be honest, I hated myself too,' she indicated her body under the bed-clothes. 'My useless bones and my weak muscles. After the accident, I was so dependent on others. Me, so used to being in control of my life.' She laughed mirthlessly. 'It was horrible.' She pronounced the word with French inflection. It summed up the awful accident and its aftermath.

'And now?' Jenna ventured.

Lisette closed her eyes. Her lids were pale crêpe. Her hair was colourless, plastered to her skin from sweating and Jenna could clearly make out the shadow of her skull under her face. She shivered. Was Lisette more ill than they thought?

She rose to fetch a clean pillow, when Lisette spoke again.

'I am what I am. No amount of physiotherapy can change that. I am trapped.' The words were bleak.

'You can change!' Jenna cried. 'You can't give up.'

'You are a dear girl,' Lisette said. 'You look surprised that I call you that. My temper isn't always the best but I do care about you. All of you.'

'If you care, then you must change. You must look forward,' Jenna argued.

'I'll try. Is that sufficient?' Lisette's voice was fainter.

'You're exhausted,' Jenna said contritely. 'You must sleep now. Here, I'll slip this pillow under your head and straighten your duvet.'

'Will you stay here beside me? I don't want to be alone.'

'Of course. I'll sit here all night. Don't worry.' Jenna pulled up her chair close by the bedside and held her stepmother's delicate hand.

Lisette was soon asleep, her breaths even and slow. The fever had broken and Jenna hoped she was on the mend.

The paramedic had warned she would need good care and a week or so of recovery from the virus. It was too bad that tomorrow was the television shoot for Gus's commercial. She desperately wanted to be there but Lisette was more important. She couldn't leave Donna to cope with her mother all alone.

10

In the end it was Shelley who stayed behind. Lisette was adamant she needed her. In her weakened state, no-one wanted to argue with her and so, with scarcely hidden annoyance, Shelley took Jenna's place on the chair in the bedroom.

Donna ran to and fro with pots of tea and capsules of medicine at Shelley's commands. She was to arrive later at Thornley once Lisette was settled for the day. Even Shelley didn't mention the day's television shoot in front of her mother.

Jenna was exhausted. She ran a comb through her hair, damp from a piping hot shower. The shock of the hot water had helped wake her but there were dark circles under her eyes. She was determined not to miss the day's events at Thornley, even if she ended up falling asleep in the middle of them! She felt a moment's sympathy for Shelley who was going to miss her starring part in the commercial, but Lisette's comfort was top priority and even Shelley appeared to bow to that.

Three cups of strong coffee later, and wrapped up against a bitterly cold, dark day, Jenna was ready. The car arrived and she was happy to find Gus in it as the chauffeur politely opened the rear door for her.

'Good morning,' Gus said. He looked fresh and energetic, dressed in a thick, black ski coat and dark trousers. Beside him Scout sat alert, cocking an ear in welcome. 'And how's the patient today?'

'She's improving, thank goodness.'

'That's good news. Where's Shelley? We must get going. The media lot will be there already. The Russells have opened Thornley to them.' There was a note of boyish eagerness in Gus's voice.

'Shelley isn't coming.' Jenna explained why.

'That's too bad but completely understandable on Lisette's part. She and Shelley are very close. Which leaves us with the problem of who's going to play the bride in the advert. Let's ponder that as we drive.'

Gus knocked on the glass partition and the chauffeur nodded. The car glided off smoothly on the road to Thornley House.

He reached for her hand and Jenna felt a familiar thrill as their skin touched. His hand was large and warm, the fingers calloused from his recent work at Thornley.

She nestled into him as far as the seat belt would allow, content to be there with him and to love him quietly. Scout pushed between them and she moved back laughing. He grinned, letting his tongue loll out.

'You win this time, old chap,' Gus said, pulling the little dog's ear playfully, 'but on the way back it'll be different . . . '

Jenna felt like a school girl in love. It

was silly but delicious. She anticipated the run back in the car and being near Gus with a heady delight.

All her senses were heightened around him. She smelt his subtle cologne, the freshly laundered shirt he wore, even the leather polish of his winter boots. She heard the faint rasp where his chin met his shirt collar, his stubble still there though he was freshly shaven. He was a man who had a five o'clock shadow all day, his colouring was so dark.

She longed to taste his lips and wondered if he would kiss her today. It was unlikely given that Thornley would be full to bursting with people. They wouldn't have any time alone together. They hadn't announced that they were a couple, which went along with taking things slowly, but Jenna wished she could display affection for him in public. Would Gus mind?

She happened to glance down at his hand and did a double take. His left hand was bare. He'd removed his wedding ring. He was staring out the window of the car at the bleak landscape and didn't notice her astonishment. Jenna quickly looked away.

What did it mean? Did it have to mean anything? Perhaps he'd been gardening and took it off to keep it safe. Even as she thought that, she knew it was nonsense. No-one gardened in the winter. Housework then. Gus had a housekeeper at Bennybank so that was unlikely too.

She gave up. If it was important then he would tell her.

*　　*　　*

The great driveway at Thornley was packed with cars. People were crunching their way across a thin layer of crystal, icy snow to the big house, all in good spirits and chatting and laughing as they went.

Gus's chauffeur brought the car to a halt right outside the front door so they could escape the bitter blast of air which nipped the fingers and blocked the nose.

Inside they were hit by the opposite climate, a jolly warmth from fires and bodies and the rich smell of mince pies and mulled wine.

Gus was greeted by Alice Russell and ushered through to the main living-room. Jenna shed her coat and it was taken by a waiter. Staff had been hired for the day and young waitresses were darting here and there with trays of drinks and little cakes. Jenna recognised her own baking being offered about as the party got underway.

'Jenna! There you are. What took you so long?' Ann cried, pushing her way through the throng expertly. She was a regular party goer and used her height and willowy slimness to her advantage in crowds. 'Isn't this fantastic?'

'I had no idea Gus had invited so many people,' Jenna said, moving out of the way of a couple who were whispering together and moving as one towards the living-room, oblivious of everything around them.

'Yeah, it's quite something. There's the TV crowd of course, but Gus asked Lesley to invite some of their regular agency clients. I think they all came!' Ann laughed. 'The competition's been a real draw.'

'Isn't it late to be doing an advert?' Jenna said. 'It's only a couple of weeks until Christmas and the competition will be over by then.'

'Not at all.' A thin woman in her late forties joined them. Her iron grey hair contrasted with her crimson lipstick and equally bright drop earrings. She pushed a leaflet into Jenna's hand.

'We aren't relying on the television advert, we circulated this leaflet around the customers as soon as Gus came up with the idea. We've had some returns already. Besides, the advert is only for local internet television and we can use it after the festive season to promote ourselves too. Who knows, it might even go viral, if we're lucky.'

'This is Lesley,' Ann said, in the brief

pause as Lesley took breath. 'She's a fireball of energy. If you want something done fast and well, ask her to organise it.'

'You flatterer,' Lesley said. A man called for her and with a quick nod, she was off at high speed.

Ann led the way to the main room. Jenna stopped in the doorway, struck by the notion that this was how Thornley should look. A large fire was crackling in the fireplace, besides which sat a brass bucket full of cherry logs for re-stocking it. The wall sconces were lit and gave off warm flickering light into a room of guests who were clearly enjoying themselves.

She could imagine parties in the past and whimsically felt the house was happy to be full of life again. The windows were the only dark places in the room. Even though it was the morning, there was little light coming in and the sky was heavy with swathes of dark grey ominous cloud.

A woman in a green dress leant over

and pulled the curtains closed. She had a clipboard and headset and Jenna guessed she was in charge of the media team. Sure enough, she clapped her hands for silence.

It took a while for the hubbub to subside until only the couple that had pushed past Jenna were still whispering. After a discreet cough from a neighbour, they stopped too.

'OK folks, we're ready,' the woman in green said. She had a sharp, American twang which struck an odd note in the old-fashioned setting. 'Can we get the bride and groom in place please.'

There was an expectant murmur in the audience. The woman waited only a second before shouting impatiently, 'Come on guys, we've a tight schedule to stick to!'

'Clarrie, we're missing a bride due to family problems,' Gus said apologetically.

Clarrie's mouth tightened peevishly. 'No bride, no show. Heck, we may as well pack up and go right now. I need

207

to know these things, Gus. You can't just spring them on me last minute. Wanna tell me what we do now?'

Ann stepped forward. 'No need to panic.'

Clarrie gave her a nasty look as if to say she never panicked. Who did she think she was?

Ann smiled placatingly. 'We've got a replacement bride. Haven't we Jenna?' She grabbed her friend and pushed her towards a frowning Clarrie.

'Okaaay.' Clarrie stretched the word out, looking Jenna up and down, assessing her potential. Meanwhile Jenna was giving Ann a hard stare that spoke a thousand words. What on earth was she thinking of? Ann nodded encouragingly.

'Perfect,' Gus said warmly. 'If you don't mind, Jenna, you'll save the day by standing in for Shelley.'

She could hardly say no. Jenna allowed herself to be taken off by Clarrie to a side room where a bundle of clothing lay draped over a chair.

'You're gonna have to hurry, the guys are waiting,' Clarrie said shortly. 'The dress is there.'

'I'll help you,' Ann said, shaking out a gorgeous cream silk dress from the pile.

The cool smooth material slid gloriously over her shoulders until the wedding dress hung with rich weight on her. Jenna spun round and it swished. The bodice accentuated her neat waist and was encrusted with tiny seed pearls while the full skirts were supported on frothy petticoats.

'I'll do your hair and make-up; we don't want to keep Clarrie waiting.' Ann expertly brushed Jenna's dark tresses and swirled them into a twist, leaving a few tendrils curling around her face before expertly applying just the right amount of cosmetics to lift and accentuate Jenna's delicate features.

There was a spontaneous round of applause as she walked in to the reception room where the filming would take place.

She looked for Gus ready to grin and share the joke. It was rather a bizarre way to spend a morning, after all. But when she saw him, he wasn't smiling. He had an unreadable expression and turned from her before she could make eye contact. She'd no time to worry about him as Clarrie shouted orders and a man in a black T-shirt and faded jeans gently moved her onto a spot on the floor.

'Bring on the groom!' Clarrie boomed, head down over her clipboard. She paused, fingers to her head set listening. 'What? You're kidding me,' she shrieked.

Her team shrank back as she stormed out.

'Now what?' The man in the black T-shirt asked.

'No groom,' someone else replied.

Jenna dared leave her spot to go over to where Ann was in conversation with Gus.

'The male actor's just phoned in sick,' Ann told her. 'I'm trying to persuade Gus that he should stand in.'

Gus shook his head. 'This is turning into a disaster. Not only has the actor let us down but there's a weather warning out. Look.' He showed them the website on his smartphone. A red warning patch covered the whole of the west coast of Strathclyde. There was heavy snow on the way with possibilities of drifts several feet deep. It would be much worse in the countryside, in places like Thornley.

'We can get this done,' Ann said firmly, 'but we need to hurry. Honestly Gus, you'll make a fine substitute for the groom, won't he Jenna?'

She didn't trust herself to answer. It was a weird situation. She was dressed as a bride, waiting to walk up the aisle to her husband-to-be. Gus was to be the husband. She swallowed nervously.

Gus mistook the reason and put his arm round her.

'Clarrie's bark is worse than her bite. If you're up for acting, then so am I.'

'Great,' Ann said gladly. 'I'll go and let Clarrie know it's on.'

The reception room was decorated in paper chains, sprigs of holly and various Christmas wreaths. Someone had thoughtfully provided a Christmas tree for the occasion. It sparkled with silver tinsel and delicate glass baubles, a golden star perched at the top. Everyone was crammed to the sides, craning their necks to see the action.

There was a single cameraman and a young woman who was surrounded by cables and had a large furry microphone on a long rod. Another young man was fiddling with a laptop, lost in concentration.

'Finally,' Clarrie said. 'OK, the bride stands here. Get the flower girls. Where's my groom? You're at the altar. Go!'

Jenna gripped a bouquet of flowers tightly. They had been thrust into her hand. The scent of hot house petals was overpowering. She felt light-headed. Behind her, Ann laid out the wedding dress train. Two little girls stood there too. They wore pretty lilac dresses and held posies of flowers in purple and white. As Clarrie gave the order to start the music and Jenna was expected to glide bride-like down the makeshift aisle, there was a yell. One of the flowergirls had tripped on the train and fallen on her knees. She was sobbing. Jenna lifted her up, mindless of the dress.

'Did you hurt your knees, sweetie? Shall we get a plaster?'

'For heaven's sake, get that snotty nose away from the dress,' Clarrie screeched, running towards them.

Jenna stopped Clarrie with a look and held the child soothingly, murmuring comfort until the sobs tailed off. A hanky was produced from Ann's bag and the little girl's face cleaned.

Clarrie looked furious. Jenna had calmly ignored her tantrums. She caught a glimpse of Gus at the end of the aisle. There it was again, that unreadable look. What was he thinking? He smiled then at her and it was gone. He looked so handsome in his suit, a pink carnation in his lapel to match some of the flowers in her bouquet.

The flowergirl was in place, sucking on a bonbon that Ann had given her. Peace had returned to the proceedings. This time the music started and the bride made her way to the altar without mishap.

'Cut,' Clarrie yelled.

They had to repeat it several times before she was satisfied. Then they cut to other scenes where Gus had to lift her over a mock threshold. Jenna enjoyed the sensation of being swept up in his arms and held by his strength.

'Break,' Clarrie barked.

With relief the crew stopped and a call for tea and coffee and more mulled wine went out. People mingled and chatted and the waitresses ran about with yet more trays of food. Jenna took the opportunity to change out of the impractical wedding dress back into her own party blouse and jeans.

Gus opened his mouth to speak to Jenna but Ann intervened. 'Can I borrow your bride a moment?'

'Be my guest,' Gus bowed teasingly.

'What is it?' Jenna asked, slightly annoyed at the interruption. She'd been looking forward to a chance to chat to Gus all morning.

Ann had taken her to a quiet corner of the living-room under the shelter of the enormous Thornley Christmas tree. This tree was tastefully decorated in matching glass balls and was majestic, its tip almost reaching the high ceiling.

Ann looked uncomfortable. 'It's about William.'

At that moment three women went past them, chatting loudly. Ann glanced away to where Gus was standing. Jenna didn't care to think about William. That was all in the past. It seemed so far away now. But she couldn't shake a feeling of responsibility for him in spite of that. If William needed her, she wanted to know.

'Is he OK?'

'As far as I know, apart from bugging the life out of me with his unreliability.

It's not that . . . has Gus been asking you about William?'

'Why would he?'

'Oh, no reason.' Ann took a glass of wine from a passing waitress, took a sip then put the glass down barely touched.

'What's this about? What has Gus got to do with William?'

'Look, forget it, I shouldn't have mentioned it.'

'You can't just start this and then refuse to tell me,' Jenna said. What was Ann trying to say? There was a sudden tension between the two friends. This was the closest they had ever come to an argument.

'Gus came to my flat the other morning. He asked me what William is like. Then he kind of ran off in the middle of me telling him. It was odd,' Ann said in a rush.

Jenna didn't know what to make of it. She felt a rush of annoyance at Ann for stirring things up then immediately felt bad. Ann wasn't trying to drive a wedge between her and Gus. She probably felt duty bound to tell her about what she imagined to be suspicious behaviour on Gus's part. Wasn't it most likely that he was jealous of William? Jenna wondered how he knew about him.

'Did you tell Gus about William?'

Ann shook her head. 'He already knew.'

It had to be Shelley. But Jenna couldn't work out why. What could Shelley gain from it? It was terrible to think that way but having lived with her stepsister now for a few weeks, sadly she acknowledged that it was the way Shelley operated. Everything she did or said was calculated to benefit herself.

The loved-up couple she'd passed early came up to them and Jenna didn't think about it any further.

'We wanted to say how much we love the favours,' the woman said, smiling. 'So inspiring. We think we might win the competition, don't we Murray?'

Murray, who looked ten years younger than his partner, nodded enthusiastically. 'It was Gilly's idea to enter, bless

217

her. She's so intuitive.' He gazed into Gilly's eyes.

It was true that love was blind, Jenna smiled inwardly. Murray had fair, thinning hair and thick black-rimmed glasses. They were what her granny would have called bottle glasses. He was slight and short. Gilly was his opposite. She was a plump amazon with intense corkscrew curls sprouting from her head.

'Did you meet at the agency?'

'We did indeed,' Gilly told her, holding on to Murray's arm coyly. 'Murray was my second date. Lesley was so wonderful, matching us. She knew just what or rather who I needed.' She giggled girlishly, making her breasts wobble alarmingly.

'I'd dated twenty girls before I met Gilly,' Murray boasted, 'but the moment I saw her sitting at the table in Gillan, I fell in love with her.'

'We've filled in the competition form,' Gilly went on, 'writing about our perfect first meeting and doing the tie-breaker. I'm not saying what we wrote but it's so good, we must win.'

'What's great about this dating agency is the personal touch,' Murray told them, making Jenna wonder just how many dates and agencies Murray had been to. 'Gus is a marvel. He knows all his customers and it's a welcoming place even if you aren't serious about finding love.'

'He's a lovely guy,' Gilly agreed. 'It's a shame he's single. There must be someone he could date at his agency.'

Jenna simply smiled. Soon Murray had steered Gilly away to where the buffet was in the other room and they could hear him asking her what she would like and her reply that she liked whatever he was having too.

'True love,' Ann said without irony. 'Want to grab some grub?' It was a peace offering so Jenna agreed even though she wasn't hungry.

The buffet was laid out on a long table under the windows in the reception room. There were sandwiches and wraps, salads, dips and crisps along with cupcakes, Jenna's speciality, and a selection of larger cakes she'd prepared for this event. The large jugs of mulled wine were emptying fast as the festive atmosphere continued.

The curtains in this room were open and revealed a sky which was darker and more sinister than earlier. The storm had arrived. Even as they watched there was a harsh rattle of hail against the panes. Snow followed, falling fast and gluing to the glass prettily. People were looking worried. There was a queue for coats and bags and the party dissolved in a panic.

'Folks, the weather warning has been upped to level one,' Gus shouted above the din. 'The party's over. Please take care getting home and a big thanks for coming. If you need help getting your car started, let me know.'

He had his big thermal jacket on and brandished a snow shovel. Beside him old Mr Russell held a shovel too. They were moving with the party guests out the front door and into a howling maelstrom of ice and snow and freezing cold air.

'Do you want a lift back, Jenna?' Ann asked, pulling on her coat hurriedly.

Lesley joined them, wrapped up so that only her face and earrings were visible under an enormous Russian winter hat which met with the collar of her furry coat. Jenna hesitated. It was the sensible option. If she went with Ann and Lesley now they would surely get back to the city before the storm hit properly. But what about Gus? She made up her mind.

'I'll wait here. Gus'll give me a lift.'

'Are you sure?' Ann said doubtfully. 'You'll be lucky to escape Thornley if you leave it another half hour.'

'I'm going to go and help dig the snow. Mr Russell doesn't look strong enough.'

Ann kissed her cheek. 'See you then. Take care.'

Lesley was practically pushing Ann out the door to get to the car and she waved over her shoulder at Jenna before they vanished into the whirling snow.

Jenna got her coat and shivered in anticipation. It was just as freezing and icy as she'd dreaded. She could hardly see a foot in front of her, the snow was coming down so thickly.

She put her feet in the footsteps before her and followed the trail from the other guests to the cars. There were only a couple left and Gus was digging vigorously round their tyres. Mr Russell was attempting to brush snow carpets from the windscreens. Jenna helped and her fingers were soon completely numb.

The cars' occupants waved their thanks as engines revved and mushy snow was spat from the rear tyres. Eventually the two remaining cars got moving and managed to drive slowly down the long drive way, two blots of dark colour in a landscape of pure muffled white.

They stamped their feet to get rid of the clots of snow, leaving melt water all over the rug. The warmth of Thornley was like a cosy blanket after the world outside. She and Gus had escorted Mr Russell back to the lodge house where Alice was peering out, worried about her husband. Together they'd then trudged back up to the main house.

'It's useless to call for Nick,' Gus shook his head. Nick, the chauffeur, had returned to Glasgow that morning intending to collect them much later in the afternoon. 'There's no way he'll make the journey from the city now. Looks like we're stranded here until tomorrow.'

'At least we won't starve,' Jenna joked, indicating the laden buffet table.

'I'll make up one of the guest bedrooms for you,' Gus said.

There was an awkward pause. Jenna hadn't thought that far ahead. Then it hit her. She was here alone with Gus. All night. As if he read her mind, Gus reached out for her and kissed her lightly.

'Hey, your hair is soaking. I'll get a towel.'

She sat in the inglenook, hearing him elsewhere in the house, the sound of a cupboard opening then banging shut. The double creak of a staircase under feet. The gurgle of ancient pipe work above. They were homely sounds, comforting and nostalgic. Thornley enveloped her with the sensation that it was alive and friendly. She shook her head at the fantastical idea. The storm was getting to her.

He returned, his skin glowing with the warmth in the house after the chill outside.

'If you want a hot shower, I've checked and the heater is on, thanks to Alice. Here's a towel. I've taken the liberty of leaving out some of my clothes upstairs for you to change into.'

Jenna was glad. Her jeans were soaked to the thighs from clearing the cars and the cuffs of her blouse too had absorbed drips and were damp and uncomfortable.

She hadn't visited the top floor of the house before. There were many doors leading off the main corridor but Gus had directed her to the bathroom which she found easily.

After her shower, wrapped in a large fluffy towel, she discovered the clothes he'd laid out for her in the next room.

It was clearly Gus's bedroom. The decor was masculine, neat and spare in gold and black colours. The furnishing was simple — a king size bed, double wardrobe and shelving, most of which was empty. She remembered him saying he didn't spend much time here. It was Leila's house more than his.

Jenna touched the shirt and trousers. They would be much too large for her but there was no alternative unless she wished to dress in her horribly cold, wet clothes.

She slipped on the trousers and bunched them up with her own belt. They billowed at the hips and she rolled up the legs. Then the shirt. It slipped over her arms and she buttoned it, feeling the intimacy of wearing his clothing. It smelt of the washing powder he used. A familiar scent that triggered a sensation in her skin.

She imagined him wearing the shirt, his muscular body moving beneath it. Suddenly and powerfully she wanted him. So aware of the fact they were the only two people in the house, she padded on naked feet downstairs to join him.

Gus's eyes darkened when he saw her. He attempted a light smile but a flickering muscle in his jaw gave it away. There was a pleasant tension between them, a frisson of energy that burst into electricity when he drew her towards him.

'You looked beautiful in the wedding dress,' Gus murmured, 'but I like this look even better.' He bent his head to kiss her, desire flashing in his eyes.

Jenna parted her lips in anticipation. The kiss was everything she hoped for and more. It was deep and passionate and seeking. She took a ragged breath and stepped away. It was dangerous. Outside the wind howled and the ice scattered on the glass in wavelets that grew in fury. Inside the crackle of the logs and hollow tune of the piping were heightened as they stared at one another.

'I think I'm falling in love with you Jenna,' Gus whispered. His brown eyes were liquid black at the centre, his brows drawn as if this came reluctantly and spontaneously from him.

'I love you too,' she whispered daringly. The shirt, far too large for her, slid from her shoulder. Before she could re-arrange it, he was kissing the soft curve of her neck then down her shoulder and arm. He hesitated. She felt the rough stubble of his chin, felt his warm gentle breath on the curve of her breast. She groaned. There was an ache in her, deep down that could only be assuaged by him.

'Gus,' she cried out. She couldn't articulate what she needed.

But he knew. He lifted her up and carried her up the stairs. Outside his bedroom he stopped as if emerging from a daze. He steadied her. Jenna gazed at him. Her heart pounded and her insides were molten. Why had he stopped?

'Are you sure?' he asked.

She had never been more sure of anything in all her life. She wanted him. More than that, she needed him . . . urgently.

'Make love to me,' she breathed.

Then he was kissing her again with raw passion, sliding the shirt from her body greedily and they were tumbling towards his bed as one.

11

Gus woke in the morning wondering if it had been a dream. He reached beside him and felt Jenna's soft hair and heard the sound of her gentle breathing. She was real.

He slid out of bed as quietly as he could, not wanting to wake her. Down in the kitchen he ground coffee beans and found eggs and a pan. He whistled while he worked.

For the first time since Leila died, he was absolutely, perfectly happy. He was in love with Jenna. He repeated it in his mind like a song. He hadn't expected a second chance at love but it had found him anyway. He knew Leila would be glad.

Taking his wedding ring off had been more than a gesture the other day. It had been at first a physical wrench. A ring of pale skin stood out on his finger.

It was the first time he had ever removed it since he married. Yet as he set the gold circle on his bedside table, Gus felt at peace. He would never forget Leila, she held a special place in his heart after all, but he'd discovered how elastic and encompassing love could be. There was room in his heart for a new love, just as intense and bonding — with Jenna.

'That smells good.' Jenna smiled tentatively at him from the kitchen doorway. Her hair was untamed and hung in curls around her face. She was wearing his shirt and he admired her long slender legs.

'Omelettes, house speciality.' Gus grinned.

He dropped the spatula to go to her. Jenna tilted her chin so he could place a kiss on her lips. They were warm and soft and inviting and he parted them, seeking her taste and feeling her body respond to him. He moulded himself against her, aware of her soft curves and delicate frame as heat soared between them and Jenna kissed him back hungrily. They clung together as though something would wrench them apart, both desperate for the other with a passion which rose with every second.

A black smoke rising from the egg pan jolted them. Reluctantly, Gus let her go.

They ate in the kitchen, close together at the table. Gus pulled up the blinds. The sky was a pale grey, washed out and empty of threat.

'It looks like we'll escape Thornley today. What do you want to do?'

'I'm almost sorry the storm is over,' Jenna said wickedly. They shared a smile, remembering the previous night.

'I should do my Christmas shopping later,' Gus said, thinking that anything would be fine as long as Jenna was by his side.

'Let's shop then,' she agreed, snuggling into him. 'Oh Gus, I'm so happy. I fell in love with you but I never thought you would love me back. You wanted to take things slowly but look at us now. Any regrets?'

'None. I was wrong, Jenna.' Gus kissed her lightly. 'Like a snowball my feelings for you gathered speed until it crashed in on me that I loved you. Slow isn't on the agenda.' Suddenly his kiss was no longer light. Jenna pushed against his chest playfully. 'We'd better stop now or we'll never leave Thornley.'

'And that would be a bad thing?'

He heard her rich laugh and felt again a soaring happiness. She had made a beautiful bride yesterday in the mock up wedding. His attraction to her at that moment had been intense. But her tenderness towards the little flower-girl had triggered a realisation. It wasn't simply her attractiveness that drew him. It was her kindness, her gentleness of spirit and her quiet determination too. Then it had struck him hard. He was in love. He'd only known Jenna for a few short weeks but he couldn't imagine life without her.

★　　★　　★

The city was frenetic with festive shoppers. Christmas was now looming in peoples' minds and mild panic had set in.

Jenna saw a woman simply sweep a selection of cosmetics into her basket and practically run to the checkout in the department store. She held on to Gus as they were pulled along in the streaming crowd up the sloping mall floor to the main store. Between them they had filled four bags of gifts and wrap and she was losing energy.

'Which of these do you like?' Gus asked casually, stopping outside the window display.

Jenna stared. The rings were presented on black velvet, their diamonds glinting enticingly under the display lights.

'Why? Are you . . . ?'

'Why wait? Our feelings for each other aren't going to change. I love you.'

Gus was leading her into the store

and before Jenna could think, the girl behind the counter was smoothly laying out the trays of engagement rings before her.

Was this the same man who had asked to take things slowly? It was all too sudden. Then the girl was helping to slide the cool gold onto her fourth finger. Gus was waiting. Jenna's doubts melted away. She loved him. Why wait indeed? Together they chose a slender white gold band with a single solitaire diamond. It fitted her finger perfectly.

'Keep it on,' Gus suggested. He put his arm round her as they stepped out onto the concourse again.

'What about Shelley?' Jenna stopped dead.

'What about her? I made it plain to her that I'm not interested. She's a friend, nothing more.'

Jenna knew that Shelley didn't see it that way.

'Let me at least tell her before she sees my ring,' she said. 'It'll come as a shock, whatever you told her. Shelley's not one to give up easily.' And not just Shelley, she thought. What about Lisette? She'd made it quite clear she expected Jenna to back off and leave Gus for Shelley to romance.

'OK,' Gus nodded reluctantly. 'But you tell her tonight. I want the world to know that you're mine.'

She kissed him tenderly.

'No-one could mistake it. You've got your arm quite firmly and possessively round me.' She laughed and hugged him closer.

'Sorry.' Gus looked embarrassed.

'Don't be, I love it,' she whispered, revelling in his shelter and protection.

Her mobile rang. She managed to grab it before voicemail cut in. It was Lisette.

'Darling Jennifer, where are you?' Her voice was a little quavering but stronger than when Jenna had nursed her. Her tone was warmer than she'd ever heard from her stepmother.

'I'm in town. How are you?'

'Improved, thank you. I am sitting up

in bed today. Donna has been a good nurse.'

Jenna hoped Lisette had told Donna that directly. It would do her stepsister's confidence good to get some praise from her mother for once.

'I texted Donna last night to explain about the storm and that I wouldn't be back until today.'

'Yes, yes,' Lisette said, sounding more like her old self, imperial and impatient. 'You must come home now, though. You will, won't you?'

Jenna bristled at her tone but reminded herself it was only Lisette's way. She didn't have to obey her commands.

'I'll be back soon,' she promised, deliberately vague.

There was a sniff on the other end of the line then a click as Lisette finished the call.

What was that all about? Jenna wondered.

Gus raised his eyebrows in question.

'Lisette,' Jenna explained, shoving her phone back into her bag. 'I think finally

236

my stepmother and I are getting along. Talking about my dad that night she was ill has helped. I understand her a little better now.'

'I'll drop you back home,' Gus offered. 'Sounds like she's missing you.'

'If you don't mind I'll make my own way home,' Jenna said. 'That way I can speak to Shelley before we appear as a couple.'

She slipped off her glittering ring under Gus's adoring gaze and set it back in its neat, leather box. She kissed him quickly on the lips before he could persuade her to change her mind and headed out of the mall to catch the underground train.

★   ★   ★

The Lintons' door now bore a festive holly wreath, hanging slightly askew. Donna's work, Jenna thought. She reached out to adjust it and almost fell inside as the door opened. William stood there with a lopsided smile.

12

'William! What are you doing here?' Jenna took a step back. How ironic that only a couple of weeks ago she would've been thrilled to see him standing there. Now she couldn't help a sinking feeling in the pit of her stomach at the sight of him.

'That's not much of a welcome from my girl,' William said, still smiling.

'Your girl? William, didn't you get my letter?' Not to mention that he'd been quick enough to drop her all those weeks ago up at home when it suited him! She couldn't forgive him for leaving her at one of the lowest points in her life. She had been miserable, vulnerable and ill but he hadn't cared enough to support her. Yet here he was now, looking much the same as usual with his rough haircut, denim jacket and hands slung carelessly in his trouser pockets.

'Jennifer, you're late.' Lisette stopped her wheelchair behind William in the corridor and beckoned her inside.

Jenna found herself herded into the living-room and into the armchair. Shelley greeted her with a sly smile, her glance flicking between Jenna and William with unabashed curiosity.

'So what do you think of my surprise?' Lisette said triumphantly, indicating William who shuffled his feet like an overgrown schoolboy and grinned at them all.

What could she say? The truth was she didn't want any more to do with William. She felt the hard shape of Gus's engagement ring box in her pocket. Her life had moved on into something wonderful. Hadn't she explained it all gently to William in her letter? He hadn't even deserved that grace from her after the way he'd left her but she hadn't wanted to sever ties on a sour note. She wished him well but expected them to be no more than friends at a distance from now on. To find him here in the Lintons' front room was astonishing. What was Lisette thinking? Her stepmother looked pleased and expectant.

'It certainly is a surprise,' she said faintly.

'A pleasant one, *non*? I've invited William to stay for Christmas. You two have catching up to do I'm sure.'

Shelley gave a little laugh and turned it into a badly mimed cough at Jenna's glare. Jenna was beginning to get a suspicion. She swung round to William.

'What put you in mind to visit?'

He lifted his weight from one dirty trainer to the other. She noticed he'd left rubber sole marks on Lisette's carpet.

'Your sister phoned and invited me. I was going to come and see you anyway,' he added hastily, misinterpreting Jenna's expression. 'I've missed you.'

Jenna and Shelley stared at one another. Shelley was the first to drop her eyes.

'I asked Shelley to contact William,' Lisette said. She paused briefly to mop her brow with her handkerchief, reminding Jenna that she wasn't yet fully well. Then she continued, her voice stronger. 'It struck me you might be lonely and missing your old friends. I thought . . . well, when Shelley and Gus get together you won't have many people to socialise with. William has offered to take you out and about, to pick up where you left off in the north.'

Jenna bit down hard on her lip so she wouldn't say anything she might later regret. Who did Lisette think she was, organising Jenna's life for her? She was tempted to pull out the little box and show them her engagement ring. Shelley was never going to get together with Gus and it was time she realised that. And Lisette too. Gus loved her. They were going to make a life together whatever her family thought of it. She knew she could count on Donna's support at least. But Lisette was suddenly coughing and her face pale.

'Are you OK? Do you want a glass of water?' Jenna asked with concern. She knew then that she couldn't announce her engagement. The shock of it would be too much for Lisette in her frail state of recovery.

'Yes, yes, water,' Lisette croaked.

Jenna rushed to the kitchen to pour a glass under the tap. She turned to find William had followed her. He still had the pathetic grin on his face.

'Jenna, I wasn't joking when I said in there that I've missed you. Look at you, you look fantastic. I really like your hair like that. And you've got a job. That coat looks new, too. Obviously things are going well here. The thing is . . . '

'William,' Jenna interrupted. 'Can it wait? Lisette needs this.' She brushed past him to take the drink to Lisette who drank it gratefully.

William sauntered in behind her. He stood so close that his jacket brushed her arm. She was suddenly irritated by him.

'How long are you staying?' she asked pointedly.

'As long as he wants,' Lisette said, tipping the last drop from the glass delicately. 'You are family after all Jennifer and whatever makes you happy, makes us happy too.'

'Gus and I might even invite you to Thornley for the new year,' Shelley chipped in, managing to sound both cosy and catty in the same sentence.

'Gus has organised a new year's party at Thornley with you?' Jenna asked with a direct look, knowing it couldn't be true.

Shelley flushed. 'Well, not quite, but he will.' She held her head high and pushed her magnificent dark gold hair from her shoulders. 'You should be grateful to Mummy for caring enough about you that she got William down here. The two of you make a perfect couple.'

William nodded in agreement, oblivious to the barb in Shelley's comment.

'I am tired,' Lisette announced.

Jenna thought she looked drawn. Perhaps her recuperation was going to take longer than they expected.

'Come along Mummy, I'll help you to your room,' Shelley said, touching her mother gently on the arm. 'Let's leave these two lovebirds. I'm sure they have a lot of things to talk about.'

Lisette caught hold of Jenna's hand as Shelley began to push the wheelchair along. 'I want you to be happy, Jennifer, that's all. This Gus, he is not for you. But William . . . yes, there's potential there I hope.' She patted Jenna's hand and allowed Shelley to take her away into the hall.

There was an awkward silence. Jenna wished she too could escape upstairs to her room. But William was oddly at ease. He sat in Shelley's vacated armchair with his legs crossed. He hadn't bothered to take his grubby jacket off and Jenna saw with disgust a smear of mud on one cuff.

What had she ever seen in him? Had she been so utterly desperate for companionship and love that she'd tolerated this man? Yet he had been good company at least at the start of their relationship, she remembered. As long as she hadn't needed anything from him.

'How are you?' she felt she had to ask politely.

William sighed, the inane grin slipping from his face. 'I'm glad you asked me that, Jenna. No kidding, I've been better.'

'I'm sorry to hear that,' she said, trying to keep the annoyance from her voice. 'I thought your job with Ann was going OK. What's happened?'

'Oh, the courier job, yes, I'm doing that. Not that I get any thanks for it. She's a right moaner, that Ann. Never off my back about being on time and the state of the van. Why did she give me a white van to drive if she wanted it so clean, eh? But I let it all wash over me, water off a duck's back. Gives me a chuckle when she gets so furious. Me, I just whistle.'

'You should be grateful to Ann for giving you the job in the first place,' Jenna said sharply.

William put his hands up in mock surrender. 'I am but she doesn't need to rub my nose in it constantly, does she? What's her problem anyway?'

Jenna sighed and sat down. He hadn't changed one bit. The world owed him, that was William's take on life.

'So, if it isn't the job, what is the problem?' she asked reluctantly. It seemed the only way to bring their meeting to a speedy end. She longed to lie down on her bed in peace, slip her engagement ring onto her finger and dream of Gus Stanton.

'You got yourself a job, Shelley says,' William said, ignoring the previous question. He sat forward eagerly. 'She's a posh bird, isn't she? Looks like an ice queen but turns out to be a chatty lass.'

Jenna wondered just how 'chatty' Shelley had been on the phone to William. What had she told him and why?

'I'm baking again,' she nodded. 'It's not permanent but it'll see me through until the new year.'

She hadn't planned beyond that but with a warm rush she realised that she wasn't alone any more. Gus would be there with her and together they would discuss the future. She would work, that she did know. She couldn't imagine not working, even if she was Gus's wife and had no need of the income.

'Shelley says you're working for a millionaire. Is that right?'

'Does it matter? He's wealthy, yes, but he made his own money through sheer hard work and determination.'

There was a message there for William, if he cared to listen.

'Do you get along with him? Are you pally, like?'

'What's this all about, William?' Jenna asked impatiently. 'It's nice to think you care about my life but what's really on your mind?'

'Hey, that's not very nice,' William said, his tone rising. 'Am I not allowed

to ask you about yourself? Seems
you like delving into my life. Two-way
street, Jenna.'

'To be honest I don't much care what
you do now. I made it quite clear in my
letter that we are finished as a couple.
Which you'd already made plain to me
when I had to sell the shop, if you
remember,' Jenna retorted.

'OK, OK. Let's calm down.' He
stood up and paced the room, not
meeting her eyes.

Jenna waited with annoyance. What
was coming?

'Thing is, I need seven hundred
pounds and I need it now,' William said
in a rush.

'What!' Jenna leapt to her feet too.

'It's not that much,' he said defen-
sively.

'Not that much,' she echoed incredu-
lously. 'What on earth have you done?'

He did his shuffling trick. It had once
been an endearing behaviour, many
months ago, but now it really made her
want to slap him.

'I borrowed some. Then a bit more. With the interest, it started mounting up.' He shrugged.

Jenna shook her head in disbelief.

'Nobody has that kind of money to simply hand over to you.'

A sly look spread across his face. 'Not many people, no.'

'Did you ask your mum?'

He snorted. 'She's not even speaking to me now. Says I've wiped her savings out. It's not true, she's just mean with her cash, and me her only son and all.'

'Who else did you ask?'

There was a pause, then, 'Ann.'

'You didn't. How could you have the cheek to ask your employer?' Jenna was horrified.

'I'm desperate. Come on, Jenna, you must have a bit stashed away. I'll pay you back.'

'No you won't. You never do. Anyway I've no savings yet. I don't know anyone who could lend you that kind of cash.'

'But that's where you're wrong. You do know someone,' William said. 'Your millionaire boss.'

Jenna was stunned. 'You seriously want me to ask Gus to give you seven hundred pounds. Just like that, with the snap of my fingers. Are you mad?'

'You don't get it, do you? If I don't pay up, then some goons are going to be visiting and it won't be for tea and cakes.'

'No,' Jenna said firmly. 'This time, no. I can't help you.'

A tide of crimson washed over his jaw as he gritted it tightly. His fists bunched and his whole body shook.

'It's all your fault,' he roared, making her jump. 'You were the one who told me I needed to get a business. That I shouldn't rely on odd jobs to get by. So I took your advice, didn't I? I bought a couple of vans so I could set up as a courier. More fool me, eh. It's your fault!'

She didn't know what to think. Maybe William was right. She had kept on at him, hadn't she, about getting training or a business . . . getting on in the world? Finally he'd done what she had recommended. He was right. It was her fault he'd landed himself in debt. Once more she'd have to help him out. With a sick feeling in the pit of her stomach, Jenna realised she'd been here before — supporting William emotionally and financially. But what else could she do? She couldn't abandon him when he was desperate. Yet she felt as if she was standing on the edge of a precipice and with one step would fall, spinning and spinning into space.

'I need to think,' she whispered, her throat parched.

As William muttered darkly under his breath, Jenna fled from him to the sanctuary of her room. She needed to be alone, her head was swirling.

Dinner was a silent affair. Jenna was only too aware of the reproachful looks cast by William as he sat opposite. Lisette appeared tired and listless and Shelley was missing. Donna had made an attempt at small talk but subsided into silence when there was no response. Jenna ate as quickly as she could without being rude and made her excuses.

★　★　★

The taxi dropped her at the front entrance of Bennybank. At another time she would have been curious about Gus's townhouse but tonight she could focus only on William's problems. His words, flung angrily at her, ran through her head.

It's all your fault! He was right. She had advised him to get proper employment. She felt guilty that because of her he was now in a state of dreadful debt. No matter what her feelings for him were or weren't, she couldn't walk away from it. She had to help him. She had no option but to ask Gus for a loan. There was nowhere else she could get that kind of money. Surely Gus would be amenable? He would understand why she had to ask, wouldn't he? And she would pay him back, she would

252

make that clear to him.

The longer Jenna stood at the front door of Bennybank, the more she managed to convince herself that she was doing the right thing. She had put her engagement ring back on her finger and it sparkled encouragingly in the lamplight. Gus loved her. Of course he would help. She needed to do this to finally get William off her back.

'Jenna, what a nice surprise!' Gus's face lit up when he saw her. He ushered her into the warmth of his house. 'I was going to call on you but this is great. Have a seat and I'll get us a drink.' He kissed her lightly and left her in a comfortable living-room, where Scout lay asleep, nose on paws.

She couldn't relax enough to sit. Padding round, it was obviously a masculine room. The furniture was dark wood with a glass top coffee table in the centre. There were none of the fripperies that a woman might add such as colourful cushions or pretty table lamps. There were computing magazines scattered on the coffee table and a mug of cold coffee.

Gus's laptop lay open with its screen saver flickering. There was a loneliness to the scene which touched her. She reminded herself that soon Gus would no longer live alone because she would be with him. She wondered when they might marry and where they would live before William and his problems sliced back into her musings.

She waited until Gus had laid out the glasses and opened a bottle of wine. Nervously she accepted a drink and joined him in a toast to their future. She took a large sip and coughed as it went down the wrong way.

'Hey, ease up on the speed,' Gus said gently. 'We've all evening ahead of us.'

She was tempted then not to say anything about the cash and William. It sounded so lovely. She could spend the evening with Gus, drinking wine, listening to soft music and talking to him. There was still so much they didn't know about each other, so much to find out.

'Is there anything wrong?' Gus asked, his brown eyes kind and concerned.

How she loved him at that moment, strongly and sweetly. She couldn't believe she'd found such a caring, loving man to share her life with.

Now that he'd asked, she knew she had to tell him what was haunting her.

'I don't know how to start,' she said truthfully.

'Whatever it is, we can solve it.' He reached for her hand.

'OK.' She took a deep breath. 'I need to ask you for a favour. It's not for me, it's for a friend.'

'If I can help, I will.' He squeezed her fingers gently.

'I need seven hundred pounds.' It came out starkly and seemed to echo in the still room.

There was a silence. She wondered if he'd heard. She was going to repeat it until she summoned the courage to look at him. A chill gripped her heart.

Gus's face was stone.

'Gus?' she whispered.

He said nothing. Jenna swallowed. Her mouth was dry. She tried to explain. 'It's only a loan. I'll get paid back. I'm sorry but I've no-one else to ask.'

'So you thought of me? How convenient that you met me. Is that what you calculated? That I've got so much money I'd be a good bet?' The icy sarcasm in his voice cut her to the core. She'd never heard him speak so bitterly.

'No, no, that's not what happened,' she said desperately. 'I fell in love with you.'

'Did you really? Was it easier, knowing I'm rich? It must have been a comfort to you when you were destitute, that I was attracted to you. I played right into your little game.'

She winced at the coldness in him. He looked at her as if she was a stranger. Worse than that, a stranger that he hated.

'I'm sorry, forget I asked. It was wrong of me,' she cried, wanting only that his eyes would warm again for her. She reached out to him but he stepped back.

'You're as bad as Kate,' he snarled. 'Shelley was right, you're a little gold digger. I was a fool to believe in you. She said you'd leeched your previous boyfriend of his money. Well, I'm not such an easy touch, Jenna. I've been burned before but I've learned from it. Get out! I never want to see you again.'

'Please let me explain. You've got it all wrong.'

'Just go.' When she didn't move, frozen by the terrible events, he barked, 'Go!'

Jenna fled, her tears blurring her vision as she ran into the night away from Bennybank and away from the only man she'd ever loved.

She slowed after a bit to a walk, wiping her tears away with a trembling hand. What had she done? She'd lost him.

She tried to calm herself, to analyse what had happened. The bitingly cold air helped crystallise her thoughts.

Her footsteps took her towards the river; she could hear its babbling as it rushed carefree along the channel out of the city and eventually into the sea.

There was an old church to her left behind high iron gates. She wouldn't have noticed it but for the hoot of a hunting owl. She turned left and pushed tentatively at the gates. They opened without a creak and she slipped inside.

There was something strangely comforting about the church. It was clearly very old and it felt peaceful standing there. She sighed. She needed peace and calm from her turmoil right now.

She followed a path along, seeing the outlines of gravestones and a fringe of old, gnarled trees. There was a stone angel in a little clearing, her head caressed by the branches of overhanging oaks. Jenna felt a great calmness soak into her. She was unafraid there in the cloak of the night.

In the distance beyond the clearing, she glimpsed city lights and the far railing of the cemetery. A bus went by. She could easily grab a taxi or get on a bus back to the Lintons. But first, she wanted to sit and think.

Ignoring the cold, Jenna sank down onto the base of the angel which was just wide enough to form a little seat. There was an inscription on its column but it was too dark to make out the words.

She tried to make sense of what had happened. Gus had been so coldly angry with her. She was stunned. It had come out of nowhere. She had hit a nerve, that was clear. What had he said? He'd accused her of being like Kate. Who was Kate? And what had she done to Gus? Then he'd mentioned Shelley.

Jenna couldn't believe it. She huddled into her coat, under the shelter of the angel. Shelley didn't like her much but to tell lies about her to Gus was despicable.

She hadn't leeched on William. It was the other way about! She'd lent William so many small amounts of money and some larger loans too. She couldn't afford it when her bakery was failing and if she was honest, it had tipped the balance and helped force her out of business. Oh, if only she hadn't tried to help him one last time.

With a sudden chilling clarity she realised she'd fallen right back into her old emotional habit with William, helping him and lending to him when she couldn't afford it. And look what it had cost her — Gus's love.

That wasn't the real me, she thought urgently. *What a fool I've been.*

'What will I do?' she asked out loud into the night. She rubbed away fresh tears. She'd lost all she cared about. She couldn't face Gus again. She wouldn't be able to continue working for him now either. She might as well pack up her belongings and go . . . but where? There was nothing for her in the North, but continuing to live in the same house as Shelley was impossible, too.

A breeze rustled the remains of the dead leaves at the foot of the angel. It was oddly mild compared to the cold air around her. Jenna's head cleared and her spirits lifted. She still had no solution to her problems but she had found a courage to go on. She stood up. The breeze had vanished as suddenly as it came. There was an air of hush and expectancy.

'Now I'm being ridiculous,' she told the angel. 'So I'll go home. Tomorrow I'll start again. I don't know how but maybe it'll be clearer to me then.'

* * *

'Where have you been?' Ann asked impatiently. She was at the Lintons when Jenna returned, having caught a late city bus with no bother. Ann was buzzing with energy as usual and followed Jenna upstairs chatting non-stop, pushing her in the back when she

261

stopped on a stair.

'Come on, I've got fantastic news. I can't wait to tell you.'

'Tell me.'

'Not until we're out of earshot of the lovely Shelley. Hurry up, won't you. Shut the door!'

Ann was practically hopping from foot to foot on Jenna's bedroom carpet. The tiny room was really too small for two people, especially when one was as tall and agitated as Ann.

'I'm quite tired,' Jenna said weakly, hoping Ann would take the hint. She wanted nothing more than to sink into her bed, pull the duvet over her and escape the horrid day. But Ann was blissfully unaware of her friend's distress. She was pulling a piece of paper from her bulging handbag and waving it excitedly.

'I'm your fairy godmother. You shall go to the ball, my dear.'

'What on earth are you talking about Ann?'

'The competition, silly. You and Gus

have won. Well, nearly. Here's the thing . . . ' Ann sat on the bed beside her. 'The advert was uploaded after the party onto the local online television station and there was a flood of emails with competition entries and lots of good catchlines — who'd have guessed so many couples would want to get married on Christmas Day. Mind you, winning a whole wedding would encourage a lot of folk. Plus of course the leaflet had been circulated before that too. Lesley showed me the results. Anyway, I put in an entry for you and Gus.' She ignored the faint cry from Jenna and carried on. 'Lesley is the judge and she agrees it's very romantic that the owner of the dating agency should be about to get engaged. She chatted to some of the regulars and they all agree that Gus and you should win the prize. It includes the wedding dress, the bridesmaids' dresses, the honeymoon, the whole caboodle!'

'You didn't know we were getting engaged,' Jenna said. 'I didn't know, so how could you?'

Ann laughed pityingly. 'Jenna dearest, it's pretty obvious the way Gus feels about you. Did you see his face when you walked up the aisle?'

She grabbed her friend's left hand and pointed at the diamond.

'Are you going to tell me I'm wrong?'

Jenna looked at Ann and burst into tears.

13

Gus and Scout were walking. They had been walking for a long while. They had followed the footpath which ran alongside the river and kept going. The snow had gone, leaving a grey landscape, muddy with slush. It matched Gus's mood.

He'd spent days and days holed up at Bennybank, not venturing out once. He'd worked constantly, turned the landline and his mobile phone off and focused on his projects, refusing to dwell on what had happened with Jenna.

When the living-room filled with crumpled balls of paper and half consumed cups of coffee, he simply moved his laptop and notepad into the study.

He'd eaten from the fridge, defrosting ready meals in the microwave or ordering home delivery takeaways and tasting none of it.

Finally, he'd felt the beard growth on his chin and the crunch of discarded containers under his feet in the kitchen and decided enough was enough. After a shower and a shave, he'd called for Scout and headed out into the dull city.

'That's it old chap, get rid of the cobwebs,' he said, trying to be cheerful.

Scout raised doggy eyebrows briefly as he trotted along. His tongue lolled out and he was panting.

'You're right. I shouldn't pretend. I'm not happy at all, Scout. I keep thinking about her. I can't believe I was taken in by her sweet act. Am I a fool? First Kate, then Jenna. What's wrong with me?'

Scout barked to keep him company until he saw a movement in the undergrowth and leapt in to investigate. Gus was left with his thoughts, none of them pleasant.

What had Jenna said? I need to ask you for a favour. I need seven hundred pounds. What she couldn't know was that she'd echoed uncannily Kate's words the first time she'd wheedled a loan out of Gus.

Kate hadn't had the brazen cheek to ask for a large amount the first time. Small sums, salted away under sweet reasoning and apologetic, appealing glances. All leading up to the finale where Kate and huge sums of Gus's hard earned cash had vanished overnight. And now Jenna. The same request for a smallish amount of money. No doubt followed by more. Jenna! He would've sworn she was different, that she was genuine. He'd put his ring on her finger and promised to spend the rest of his life with her.

He stopped on the riverbank and rubbed his face, staring at the brown water without seeing it. The awful part of it was he still loved her. He couldn't switch his feelings off. He doubted they would fade in time. They were too powerful.

Had she faked her kisses? Had she

acted a part of a caring, kind young woman with vulnerable large grey eyes? She'd come across as a girl who needed love . . . and he'd fallen for all of it. Fallen for her heavily and irrevocably.

Scout burst out of the willow thicket. He sat at Gus's feet patiently. Gus hunkered down to the dog, picking sodden burrs from his wiry coat. He stayed crouched even after Scout wriggled out and scampered up the path intent on chasing an unwary wood pigeon.

Something else that Jenna had said came back to him. *It's not for me, it's for a friend.* A friend? Was that a ploy too? Or had he not really listened to her? He'd reacted to the key words 'favour' and 'seven hundred pounds', going off like tinder as he was reminded of Kate.

Slowly Gus stood up. Around him swept the brown swathe of river and beyond the lights and noise of the city. The pigeon had flown on whispered feathers out of Scout's reach and the dog was returning to him.

All this passed in detail in Gus's head but all he could think was that he needed to find Jenna. He needed to let her explain. He owed her that at least.

★ ★ ★

Jenna wandered listlessly through the tiny hall and through to the living-room. Her feet made hollow sounds in the silent flat. How many days had she been here now? It was beginning to feel like a prison. The main feature of the living-room was a large window through which she could see the grey ocean and a rain-lashed promenade. A few seagulls circled on the air but there was no-one about. Everyone would be holed up in their homes preparing for the festivities to come.

Ann had insisted that Jenna have the keys to her flat in the Highlands.

'I'm not going back there until the new year,' she'd said. 'Of course you must stay there. Where else would you go? I'd ask Lesley if you could stay with us but you've told me not to.'

'It's too close,' Jenna said. 'I have to get out of Glasgow. I can't bear the thought of bumping into Gus in town.'

'Oh Jenna . . . please, please try again. Go back to Bennybank and speak to Gus. Explain what you meant and the pressure William put you under. That William, I could kill him!' Ann punched the air furiously. 'I'm sacking him today.'

'You can't do that,' Jenna cried. 'Then he'll have no income at all to pay his debts back.'

'Serves him right. Oh, don't look at me like that — I won't actually sack him. But I'm going to make him pay for what he's done to you. No more leniency from me. One more mistake, one more delayed delivery and he's out on his ear. Now promise me you told him you can't help him, right?'

Jenna nodded. 'I did. In the end. After Gus's reaction, I understood what I'd done. I told William that he was on his own and that I couldn't and wouldn't help him financially ever again.'

'And?'

'It didn't go down well. I'd no idea he'd such a rotten temper. He's moody and prone to tantrums but this was . . . something else. Anyway, when he calmed down and saw I was serious, he just packed up his kitbag and stormed out of the house. Turns out he has a mate or two in the city to doss down with, as he put it. I sincerely hope I never have to see him again.'

'How did Lisette take it? From what you said, she was keen to do a little matchmaking between the two of you.'

Jenna managed a watery smile. She'd done nothing but cry since she'd fled Gus's house. The next day she'd had an unpleasant argument with William and then finally run to the sanctuary of her best friend. Luckily Lesley was out at a party and Ann was there dressed in an old bathrobe with her hair up in a pony tail, munching on crisps with the blare of the telly in the room behind her.

'She accused me of sending William away and spoiling my chances. And then I was so distraught that I told her straight how I felt. About William's demands and how much in love with Gus I am. The whole story.'

Ann stopped with a handful of crisps mid-way to her mouth. 'Wow, that's my girl.'

'I didn't wait to see her reaction. I turned on my heel and ran straight to you.'

Ann got up from the sofa and went to a row of hooks above a corner cabinet. She came back with a bunch of keys.

'Stay up there as long as you like. It'll be rather squashed once I get back in January but we'll be OK.'

Jenna thanked her with heartfelt gratitude. She promised herself she'd be out of Ann's flat by the time the new year arrived, although as to what she was going to do with the rest of her life, she hadn't a clue. For the moment it was enough that she had a bolt-hole to hide in.

She let herself in quietly at the Lintons'. Funny how she'd never considered it 'home'. Perhaps she'd always known deep down that she was an intruder, an outsider. All her plans for getting to know her family and building loving bonds with them had come to nothing. She tiptoed upstairs and packed her few belongings as quickly as she could.

'I hope you're not going to run out on us without saying goodbye.' Donna looked distressed as she stood in the doorway, hugging a shawl round her.

Jenna's face coloured. That was exactly what she was planning to do.

'Sorry, I couldn't face you all. I've done enough explaining about William and Gus.'

Only she hadn't managed to explain to Gus himself. If only he'd let her tell him the whole story. He'd been so incredibly angry with her. She felt her eyes well up again and swiftly focused on latching her suitcase, hoping Donna wouldn't notice.

But Donna had wet eyes too.

'I'm really going to miss you,' she said tearily. 'You're like another sister to me.'

'That's the nicest thing anyone's said to me,' Jenna said, giving her a fierce hug. 'I have to go but I'll write to you. You'll write back, won't you? And visit?'

'Try and stop me.'

In the end, Donna persuaded her to stay the night and she and Stewart gave her a lift to the train station the next morning.

Shelley was triumphant and didn't bother to try to hide it. She had won. Jenna was leaving not only their house but the city too, leaving the coast clear for her to make contact with Gus and win him back. All this was writ clear on her face as she waved farewell to Jenna.

Lisette was quietly upset when Jenna went but pride wouldn't allow her to admit her mistakes. Instead, she retreated into cool formality which hurt Jenna more than she'd imagined. She'd become fond of her prickly stepmother in the weeks she'd lived there. But she didn't let her hurt show.

She was glad of Stewart's pleasant company as he lifted her bags into his car, talking inconsequentially. He and Donna waved vigorously until the train was out of sight.

★   ★   ★

And now here she was. The flat was bare, clean and tidy as Ann had left it. There were no decorations or any hint of the festive season. But that was alright. She hadn't the heart or the energy to hang tinsel and glass bells. All she wanted to do was sleep for a fortnight. Once Christmas was over she would emerge and sort herself out.

She went into the tiny kitchen and made herself a cup of tea. But she was restless. Despite her desire for sleep, she couldn't seem to settle. In the end, she put on her thickest coat and rammed a woolly hat on her head. It wasn't as if anyone was going to see her, she reasoned, so fashion needn't matter. She'd go for a brisk walk along the promenade and wear herself out. Then maybe she could rest and not think of Gus.

The rain hit her face as soon as she left the shelter of the flat. Great icy droplets slammed almost horizontally onto her. She ran across the cobbled street and onto the promenade. A row of unhappy, drenched gulls flew up and away, squawking their displeasure.

Beyond the railings the sea roared and lashed against the pebble beach. In the near distance, she saw breakers sweep over the rails and across the promenade, flinging seaweed like confetti onto the road.

No wonder no-one was out. She tucked her frozen hands into her pockets and set off up the coast towards the lighthouse on the tip of the peninsula. It was a good half-hour walk to get there but she had all the time in the world.

The great thing was that in the

blustery, horrid conditions, she couldn't think. She concentrated on the pain in her cheeks, blasted by the rain and the wind, and the tip of her nose which felt like an icicle.

The wind roared in her ears and whipped her hair into her eyes. She was bent almost double pushing into it. There was an exhilaration to pitting her strength against nature, a perverse pleasure in trying to beat it. She screamed into the gale, abandoning herself to the moment.

The lighthouse flashed and she looked up, startled. Darkness was encroaching, it was the absolute depths of winter after all and daylight hours were short and precious.

For a moment she glimpsed a figure set against the white painted exterior of the lighthouse but the next minute all was obscured by a wave, bigger than the others, pouring deliriously over the concrete and soaking her feet. She cried out loud in shock and heard the water laugh as it scraped back over the stones for another round.

Had she imagined someone else out in the raw day? She strode on, determined to reach the lighthouse and its twinkling beacon.

There was no lighthouse keeper these days, it had been automated some years back . . . so who was it? A figment, conjured out of mist and shadows perhaps? But then she saw there was someone, a man, walking in the opposite direction, headed straight for her.

Unlike her, he had the wind at his back and was been guided along by a strong hand. Their paths would almost certainly collide. Just as she thought to politely step off the narrow promenade path to let him by, Jenna did a double take.

'I've found you,' Gus cried into the wind. He didn't stop his progress for a second, simply sweeping her up in a bear hug and sealing his warm lips to hers without explanation or apology or any other word.

She didn't protest. She clung to him

like a limpet to rock and kissed him back, fiercely demanding, ignoring the rain that lashed them and stung them and ran in rivulets between them.

For a long, endless moment they wrapped themselves as one in the storm, giving and taking of each other. Then Gus raised his head, his dark hair wet and spiky, his brown eyes seeking forgiveness.

'Jenna, I thought I'd lost you. I never gave you a chance to tell me. I'm so sorry.'

His words were almost lost in the bellowing winds.

She shook her head. 'Let's go home.'

★   ★   ★

Ann's flat looked different. It wasn't cramped, it was bijoux she decided as she curled up against Gus on the two-seater couch. He caressed her hair, kissed her lips and pulled her close, warming her more than her hot shower had done.

'I blew up at you,' Gus tried to explain. 'My experience with Kate had scarred me more than I realised.' He had told her all about his short relationship with Kate and the after-math of it. 'It was unforgiveable and my stupid pride wouldn't let me acknowl-edge I was wrong. That's why it's taken me so long to find you.'

'How did you know where I was?' Jenna snuggled in closer, revelling in his scent, his warmth, the roughness of his stubbled chin, the feel of his cotton shirt, all of it.

'Ann told me. Unfortunately I was in such a hurry that by the time I got here I couldn't remember the flat number. I had the vague notion of walking up and down the coast path in case I saw you in a window. That's all I knew, that Ann's flat faced the sea.' He shrugged.

'I'm so sorry I asked you for that money,' Jenna said again. 'I felt guilty that William had borrowed because of my advice.'

Gus silenced her with a kiss.

'Forget it. And forget him. He's an unfortunate soul. If Ann does sack him, I'll give him a job in the restaurant kitchens if he'll take it. That's the only help he'll be getting from us.'

Us. The word had a lovely ring to it, promising to banish loneliness forever.

'Are you cold, my love?' Gus asked, stroking her arm and raising goose bumps along her skin with his touch. 'Because if you are, I think I've a way to warm you up . . .'

'It's Christmas Day tomorrow,' she said, after Gus had warmed her delightfully with hot kisses. 'It's not going to be much of a Christmas here.'

'Who said we were going to be here?' he asked with a grin. 'The wind is due to die down and there's a private airstrip north of here. How do you think I got here? I've a plane ready to take us to Glasgow when you're ready.'

'Where will we go?'

'We got married once at Thornley after a fashion,' Gus said, a gleam in his eye. 'Would you consider doing it again,

281

this time for real? Ann tells me we won our own competition. It would be a shame to let it all go to waste.'

'If that's a proposal of marriage, Gus Stanton, then the answer's yes!'

14

'So you won after all. I don't know how you did it.' There was a grudging admiration in Shelley's voice. She sat watching Donna fix Jenna's bridal veil, one satin-clad foot swinging casually, the champagne silk bridesmaid dress sliding up to show her fine leg.

'You make it sound like a game,' Jenna remarked, determined not to get annoyed on this day of all days.

'It was a game of sorts,' Shelley said with a twisted smile. She came over and fixed a curl on Jenna's head that had escaped Donna's attention. 'You look OK.'

Big praise indeed from her stepsister! Jenna smiled to herself. Nothing could take the shine off her wedding to Gus.

The three sisters were in an upstairs bedroom at Thornley House, getting ready for the simple ceremony which would take place in the main living-room. There was less than an hour to go and Donna's hands were shaking slightly as she fixed the last tiny white blossom into Jenna's dark curls.

'There!' She stepped back to admire her handiwork.

Jenna was very much the winter bride in an ermine trimmed wedding gown which was antique cream velvet threaded with gold. It was Christmas Day and there was no snow but a pretty frosting to the glass windows and a sparkling ice veneer to paths and grass stems.

From downstairs came the sound of laughter as guests arrived and the occasional shriek of a violin as the live orchestral band prepared for the celebrations.

Jenna had been surprised and touched by how many of their friends wanted to celebrate with them, despite it being Christmas Day.

Donna sighed happily. 'Oh, it's so romantic. How beautiful Thornley looks today. And then you'll have a marvellous honeymoon to go on too.' She glanced at her own hand proudly. On her fourth finger there was a tiny diamond engagement ring. Stewart had proposed in the heat of the excitement at Gus and Jenna returning home and announcing they were getting married immediately.

'Have you set a date yet?' Jenna asked, knowing just how contented Donna was now with her life.

Donna shook her head. 'I'd like a summer wedding but it's going to be ages before we can actually get married. We have to save for a house first.'

'You'll still have your job with me,' Jenna reassured her. 'I'm going to set up my own bakery again, with Gus's backing.'

'I'm counting on it,' Donna replied. 'Now, how do I look?' She twirled round in her dress which matched Shelley's. Jenna had insisted she wanted both her sisters to be her bridesmaids. Donna had cried with joy at her request while Shelley had said little but not refused, Jenna had noted.

'You're in a size too small,' Shelley

commented, from her perch on the window seat.

'Ignore her,' Jenna said quickly before Donna could get upset. 'Now, listen, can you give me some advice on what to wear for something old, blue, borrowed and new? I've got a blue hanky . . . ' She pulled Donna with her to her suitcase which was spilling out onto the floor.

Trust Shelley to make a mean comment. She just couldn't help herself. Her jealousy at Donna's happiness was obvious and it came out in spiteful mutterings. How they would manage living in the same house for the foreseeable future, Jenna had no idea.

She was sneakingly glad she wouldn't have to bear it directly. She and Gus were going on honeymoon to Australia just as the competition prize described and when they returned they were going to live at Thornley.

Gus had told Jenna she could choose where their main residence would be.

She'd chosen Thornley over Benny-bank. It was less convenient for the city and commuting to work but her love for the old house was intense. She couldn't imagine living anywhere else. And Gus, who'd once looked upon Thornley as Leila's, had agreed it was a good place to set up home together.

Since the renovations, it was a fresher Thornley with a positive atmosphere promising good things for the future.

'Are you ready?' Shelley asked. They heard the music start up downstairs and a hush from the guests. Jenna's stomach clenched. She thought of Gus, waiting for her and it calmed her. It was going to be fine.

'Yes. Let's go.' She adjusted her veil and let Donna fix her short train. Shelley unexpectedly crooked her arm in invitation. She hesitated then slipped her arm into Shelley's. A peace offering, she wondered, or a temporary truce? Whatever it was, she was glad of the company as they moved carefully down the stairs and across the hall to the large room full of friends wanting to share their moment.

Most of all, there was Gus. He stood at the end of the makeshift aisle with the minister beside him. She had a sense of déjà vu especially when she glimpsed Clarrie in the crowd. But this was real, no television advert.

Gus was impeccable in his morning suit and a crimson cravat, giving hint to the season and the special nature of the day. She thought him rather solemn until he winked subtly just for her. At once, she relaxed and began to enjoy herself. It was her Gus whatever the trappings. They belonged together.

The ceremony went by in a blur as she gave the answers required and they exchanged vows and rings. All the time she was conscious of Gus's reassuring grasp of her hand, squeezing it gently when she stumbled over his middle names — why had his parents given him three! — and tightly as she said 'I do'. Then he was kissing the bride and a great cheer went up from the audience and the party proper began.

'May I have the pleasure of the first dance Mrs Stanton?' Gus asked, guiding her smoothly onto the polished wood floor where the Persian rugs had been lifted specially for the occasion.

'You may indeed, my husband,' Jenna replied, relishing the word. She couldn't resist a kiss before the dance began. He was hers entirely. It was a heady feeling, knowing they had an eternity together.

Gus swept her round the dance floor with more energy than technique then other couples were joining them. When it got too crowded to move, they decided to mingle with the guests. The party had spilled out into the hall and the other reception room where another roaring fire had been lit in the old fireplace and food and drink had been set out in an attractive buffet.

She lost Gus almost at once to an old friend who grabbed him enthusiastically. Jenna took a goblet of mulled wine from a passing waitress and sipped.

'Congratulations, best friend.' Ann appeared with a piled plate of canapés, a large glass of wine and a short fair-haired companion. Jenna immediately remembered Gareth from their double date. 'How does it feel to be a married woman?'

'Wonderful,' Jenna laughed. 'Hello Gareth, how are you? I didn't know you two were seeing each other.'

Astonishingly, Ann blushed bright red. 'I should've mentioned it but it's quite casual, isn't it Gareth?'

'So you keep telling me,' Gareth joked. 'I'm just waiting for the word to take it more seriously.'

'Really?' Ann almost dropped her plate.

Gareth caught it expertly, his rugby practice showing its worth. Jenna hid a smile. It looked as though Ann had met her match at last.

Lesley ran up. 'Guys, I've had a super idea for the next promotion for the agency. What do you think of this . . . ?'

Jenna left them to it and went in

search of Gus. But before she could find him, she was intercepted by a slight young man with thick-lensed spectacles. It was Martin . . . Mike . . . no Murray, she remembered thankfully. But where was Gilly? There was a young woman with him who was a mirror image of himself, tiny and thin with lank blonde hair and enormous framed glasses.

'So you won,' he said to her rather reproachfully. 'Gus won his own competition.'

'Sorry,' Jenna said lamely. 'We were told the agency customers insisted upon it.'

'Most of them did,' Murray agreed dolefully, 'especially Gilly and her friends.'

'How is Gilly?' Jenna asked.

He shook his head. 'We were totally wrong for each other. I'm with Heather now. She's so intuitive, we're compatible in every way. Aren't we?' He turned to his girlfriend. She nodded timidly but didn't speak. Murray steered her away, calling over his shoulder to Jenna, 'I love this agency, man.'

Jenna drifted towards the buffet, stopped every step of the way by well wishers. Even Clarrie congratulated her warmly.

At the buffet table she saw Gilly with a plate piled high with both savoury and sweet goodies. She started guiltily at Jenna's presence.

'I'm comfort eating. Murray dumped me.'

'I'm so sorry, you must be devastated.'

'Not really. It's an excuse to eat,' Gilly chuckled, cheering up as she spotted an elaborately decorated cupcake and added it to her spoils. 'Just as well me and Murray didn't win the competition. We'd have looked a right pair of fools. I'm so glad you and Gus got your dream wedding. You two deserve it. Anyone can see you're deeply in love.'

'Weren't you in love with Murray?'

'Ah, well, there's love and then

there's love,' Gilly said sagely.

'Can I interrupt?' William was there sheepishly beside her. He was wearing a too tight shiny suit and his hair was sleeked down with oil, giving him the look of a sixties crooner.

'What are you doing here?' Jenna couldn't help asking.

'Shelley invited me. I . . . I came to say sorry. I overstepped the mark a bit asking for the cash.'

'A bit?' Jenna was indignant.

'OK, a lot. Give me a break.'

'Yeah, give him a break,' Gilly breezed, offering him a meringue. She winked at Jenna.

William took the meringue and ate it under Gilly's caring gaze. Gilly nudged Jenna with her elbow in a kind of 'look at him' way.

It was Jenna's cue to go.

Through a mouthful of sweet, William said, 'I came to say goodbye. I'm going to London, there's a mate of mine there can fix me up with stuff.'

'We'll see about that,' Gilly said

softly, plying him with a chocolate profiterole.

'I run a couple of delivery vans,' William told Gilly, trying to impress her. 'It's my own business. I don't suppose . . .'

Jenna didn't bother to say goodbye. Somehow she wondered whether William would make the journey to London after all. Poor Gilly. Yet on another glance, she reckoned Gilly would be OK. William was following her dog-like to a pointed command to lay down the plates and fetch a couple of drinks. She smiled.

'There you are darling. Can you spare a minute?' Gus said. 'I've a few presents to give out to the family.'

'It's usually the other way round at a wedding,' she teased.

There was a pyramid of presents waiting for them in the front room. Despite the short notice, people had brought gifts with them. She didn't care if they had none. She had Gus.

'Now that I'm family I wanted to

spread our happiness to your sisters and mother,' he said.

'What a lovely idea.'

She followed him to where her stepmother Lisette was sitting with Donna, Stewart and Shelley. Scout lay under the table, his red festive collar sparkling with glitter. He looked up with long-suffering liquid eyes as if to say that it was beneath his dignity to sparkle so.

'Jennifer, I must add my congratulations to everyone else's,' Lisette said stiffly.

She bent to kiss the older woman's cheek. 'Thank you.'

Gus turned away to speak to Clarrie who had accosted him. She was loudly drunk and pulled him onto the dancefloor. His present-giving would have to wait.

'I confess I was not happy for you and Gus to be together,' she went on slowly. 'I had the plan for him and Shelley to marry.' She sighed with a last longing. Her shoulders went back.

'However it was not to be. I hope you will not regret it. I pray you will not.'

'I am your daughter too,' Jenna said, 'and I hope very much that you are happy for me now.'

'Tell me something. Why did you come home? It was not simply that you had to. You have friends you could have stayed with, I presume.'

'I needed to, if I'm honest. But you're right. It was more than that. I wanted a chance to get closer to all of you. And I have.'

Lisette looked at her. 'I was afraid when you said you were coming home.'

'Afraid?' Jenna was taken aback.

'*Oui.* You were a reminder of Norman, you see. I wasn't sure what that would do to me. My own emotions were so mixed when I remembered him and the accident. I was harsh to you. I'm so sorry now. Part of me wanted you to go away. If I made you work, made you unwelcome, you'd flee. But you are a very determined young lady; stubborn like Norman. You dug in your heels and demanded of me. You didn't let me have it all my own way. I admire you for that.'

The long speech had tired her. She patted Jenna's hand fondly. She didn't need to say more. The air was cleared. There was an affection there between them.

'Shouldn't you rescue Gus?' Donna suggested hesitantly.

They all looked towards the floor where Clarrie was leading him in a dance that might have been a waltz. Her loud American twang boomed out, instructing him where to step and to speed up. Gus was politely letting her drag him about through the crush of dancers.

'He's fine,' Jenna said wickedly. 'It's practice for when he insists I have to dance again.'

She was a reluctant dancer, much preferring to watch from the side. Gus had persuaded her to have a few circles of the floor as it was their own wedding but now she was glad to be out at the edge. Clarrie could wear him out on her behalf.

But Shelley rose eagerly and wove her way between couples until she reached them. Jenna watched her lean in to Clarrie. She grimaced. Was Shelley always going to try to interfere? Didn't she get it? Gus was no longer on offer. There was no need of rivalry between them. A moment later she and Gus were back, both flushed and perspiring a little.

'That woman's impossible,' Shelley announced.

Donna caught Jenna's eye and they tried not to laugh. Self-awareness was not Shelley's strong point.

Gus mopped his forehead with his handkerchief before speaking. 'Jenna and I would be honoured if we could make a few little gifts on the occasion of our wedding.' He included them all in his gaze round the table. 'I'm delighted to join the family. I have no close relations of my own, with my parents and Leila all gone.' His voice was firm, lingering only briefly on Leila's name and finding none of the old pain associated with it. He turned first to Donna and Stewart.

'Donna, you've always made me welcome at your house and in your quiet way you've been a solid and loyal friend to both me and Jenna. You've chosen a great chap to marry and as a wedding present to you both, we'd like you to accept this.' Gus passed an envelope to Donna.

She went pink at being the centre of attention but managed to open it. She gasped and showed the contents to Stewart.

'We can't accept this, Gus,' Stewart protested, trying to give the cheque back. 'It's far too generous.'

Gus shook his head firmly. 'That's for you and Donna to buy your first home together. We won't take it back so you may as well spend it.' He hugged Jenna to his side while Donna burst into tears of joy and had to be rubbed on the back by her mother when hiccups erupted too.

'Lisette,' he turned to his new mother-in-law, 'I hope you will take your present in the way it's intended.'

'What could I possibly need?' Lisette said, indicating her wheelchair.

'I have a friend who leads a top spinal team in the States. Would you be willing to let him examine you? There are great advances being made in his field. I can't promise a miracle for you but he's helped people with similar injuries walk again,' Gus said gently.

Lisette swallowed convulsively. 'I . . . I don't know. This is, comment dire . . . out of the blue.'

'I understand,' Gus nodded. 'You don't have to give me your answer now. It wasn't appropriate for me to offer before, but now I'm your son-in-law, I felt that I could.'

Shelley coughed. Gus smiled. 'I hadn't forgotten you. I was stumped for a gift but Jenna suggested designer clothes?'

Shelley shook her head. 'I'll swap the

clothes for a plane ticket to America. I'm going with Mummy when she goes for her treatment. Because you are going, Mummy. You're not wasting this chance in a million.' This last statement was said fiercely with a glimmer of tears in her eyes.

Jenna decided she'd never understand her sister. Just when she had her pegged as selfish and self-centred, she did something wonderful and astonishing and loving.

Impulsively, she grabbed Shelley and gave her a big hug. For a second it looked as if Shelley would throw her off in horror but then she was returning the hug loosely, warily, but yes, returning it all the same. They might never be best friends but they could be family.

★   ★   ★

A long while later, Gus and Jenna lay side by side on the bed in the master bedroom. Her bridal veil lay abandoned on the floor and she'd kicked her high heeled shoes off with relief. Gus had removed his bright cravat and embroidered waistcoat. The rest of the house was silent apart from the creak of old timbers as the house relaxed for the night.

'Did you enjoy our wedding, my darling wife?'

'I'll remember it forever.' Jenna curled towards him. 'Everyone else looked like they were having a good time too. Well, almost everyone.'

'Shelley?'

'That's my only regret,' Jenna said sleepily. 'I so wanted us to be friends but I don't see it happening any time soon. She was pretty much avoiding me today.'

'Don't give up too readily on her,' Gus said. He turned in towards her and stroked the hair away from her face. 'Hey, are you falling asleep on me?'

Jenna tried to lift her heavy eyelids. The emotion of the day was hitting her now but Gus had other ideas.

'It's our wedding night,' he whispered dangerously. 'I'll have to think of something to wake you up.'

He kissed her eyes and her brow and then teasingly at her lips until Jenna moaned in pleasure and her senses awakened, tingling and ready for more.

15

The invitation to dinner came out of the blue. Jenna and Donna were in full swing at the coffee shop, taking orders and practically running between the bleached wood tables with trays of drinks and plates of cakes.

Jenna stopped for a brief moment amongst the hectic activity to relish it all. The café was her dream come true. The dream had changed from a bakery to a coffee shop during discussions with Gus on their long, idyllic honeymoon two years ago.

There was a real pleasure in providing customers with the best quality teas and coffees and home baking in a pretty setting. Jenna and Donna had spent hours chatting and sketching out what the coffee shop should look like. They had finally agreed on recycled wood tables and chairs with green-checked tablecloths and olive pottery crockery. In the window they hung bunches of herbs and in the sill display, set out wicker baskets of coffee beans and a selection of their daily baking. The response was amazing. They could hardly keep up with the number of people who wanted to come inside and order from their small but delicious menu.

Jenna was seriously considering taking on more staff and trying to expand her premises. There was an empty shop next door which looked suitable to knock through to, if she could get the tenancy on it. It brought her original bakery in the north to mind, when she saw the empty shop front. She'd been in a sorry state in those days, jobless and homeless, having to flee south to Glasgow to beg shelter from her stepfamily. But if it hadn't happened, she would never have met Gus. It was weird how fate played out.

The phone rang just as a family came

in and sat down at the last empty table. Donna waved her away. 'I'll get this one, you get the call. We're out of lemon cupcakes. I'll get a batch on when I get a minute.'

Jenna nodded her thanks and picked up the receiver.

'Jennifer?' Lisette had lost none of her imperious manner but nowadays it was infused with real affection which wasn't hidden when she spoke to her stepdaughter.

'Is everything alright? Do you need me?' Jenna asked anxiously. The coffee shop was only a five minute walk on the other side of the park from the Lintons' house.

'No, no, I'm fine. You worry too much about me,' the older woman said. 'I want you and Gus and Donna and Stewart to come to dinner tonight. It's short notice I know, but you will come?'

It was a request but there was no real room for refusal. Jenna didn't mind. She found it amusing how

Lisette manoeuvred herself and everyone around her so smoothly.

'We'd love to,' she said warmly. Only once she'd put the phone down did she wonder why they were invited on a weeknight. She soon forgot about it in the crisis over the lack of cupcakes and the need to offer an especially sugary cream cake to avoid a small girl's tantrums because of it.

Gus arrived at the coffee shop at six as they were closing up for the day. She felt her heart beat faster when she saw him. She was just as much in love with him as when they'd wed and she knew she always would be.

'Thought I'd give you two a lift home,' he called cheerfully. 'We're expected at Lisette's at seven thirty.'

'Any idea what the occasion is?' Jenna asked, rattling the padlock and making sure the place was secured.

'Shelley was muttering about coming home. But she hasn't called recently,' Donna said as they got into the car.

Shelley had accompanied her mother

to America for Lisette's investigatory tests. Clarrie turned out to have family in New York and had helpfully arranged a place to stay for them. They had been there for several months before Lisette returned home with a paid nurse but without Shelley. She'd decided to stay in New York and Clarrie's brother had got her a job in an art gallery there, similar to the one she'd worked briefly in for Gus.

In one way it was a relief that Shelley had gone. She could no longer upset either Donna or Jenna with her snide remarks and barely disguised jealousy. But there was a regret that niggled with Jenna, that she'd never found a way to make Shelley like her. Maybe it wasn't possible. After all, no-one could be liked by everybody they met.

The pity of it was that they were sisters and should be closer. If only they enjoyed the same close relationship that had developed between her and Donna. Gradually she'd let the regret slide to the back of her mind and like the rest of them, she'd imagined that Shelley would never come back from the States.

Lisette opened the door to them that evening. Jenna could never quite get used to the thrill of seeing her stepmother standing. She was slow and shaky and using two walking canes but she was upright thanks to the marvels wrought by the medical team Gus had got for her.

As the evening wore on she would sit in her wheelchair but now she was not trapped in it. A much happier and relaxed Lisette had emerged as her rehabilitation went on.

'Please come in. I have a wonderful surprise for you in the dining room.'

'Mummy, don't. I'm not going to hide in there and leap out like a cheap theatrical,' Shelley drawled, appearing behind her. She'd acquired a mid-Atlantic twang somewhere over the two years and accentuated it purposefully.

'Shelley, how lovely to see you,' Jenna said, reaching out to embrace her.

Shelley stood back so she missed.

Same old Shelley then, Jenna thought miserably. But Shelley was pulling someone else into view. A tall, thin man with dark curly hair and wire-rimmed glasses.

'This is my fiancé, James,' Shelley announced proudly.

There was a moment of complete silence. James took the pause as an opportunity to shake their hands. An expensive wristwatch and cufflinks glinted in the light. Jenna noted the good cut of his suit and the designer silk shirt.

'Darling, you didn't tell me you were engaged to James,' Lisette reproached but she sounded pleased too.

'I wanted it to be a surprise,' Shelley replied, laughing. 'I only told Mummy that I was bringing a friend with me from New York,' she told them. 'James is Clarrie's older brother.'

'Congratulations.' Jenna was the first to find her voice. Dare she risk another hug and a rebuff?

But then Shelley was embracing her,

Donna, Stewart and Gus with a casual warmth, each in turn, and drawing them with her into the house, leaving James to escort Lisette, which he did perfectly in an old-fashioned, gentlemanly way.

The dinner was a success with plenty of conversation and laughter and catching up.

Lisette beamed as she looked around at her family from her place at the head of the table. Jenna had never seen her so animated and so well. The ghosts of the past had been laid to rest, she was glad to see.

There was a new photograph of her father in an ornate silver frame on the sideboard. Lisette caught her glance and nodded. 'I am finding your father once more, Jennifer. I remember only the happy times now. So, when you are in the house, you will see him in little pictures here and there. It's good.'

After the first course while the others argued over whether to leave a gap before dessert or to carry on and tuck in to the delicious cheesecake waiting on the side, Jenna excused herself. She went out into the hall, intending to check her phone for texts from Ann. She and Gareth were expecting their first child any day now and she'd promised to be there as a support to both of them.

'Marriage suits you.' She turned in surprise to find Shelley had followed her out. 'I wonder if it'll suit me half so well.'

'I'm sure it will, if you truly love James.' There was an unspoken question in Jenna's remark.

Shelley laughed but it had none of the bitter edge it used to have. 'I do love him. Very, very much. You did me a favour, Jenna.'

'In what way?' She was taken aback.

'You won Gus's heart and took my dream wedding.'

'I . . . ' Jenna started wearily to apologise but Shelley interrupted.

'It was the best thing that could've happened to me. I was so angry when I went to the States. Angry and unhappy. But then I met James and I'd never, ever felt such a powerful attraction to any guy. It took a while to dawn on me that I loved him and that he loved me back. So thank you for taking Gus.'

'Shelley . . . could we start afresh? Could we lose our history and clean the slate?'

Shelley contemplated her then pushed back her hair in a familiar gesture. She nodded slowly. 'We can give it a go.'

That was good enough for Jenna. She linked arms with her sister and the two women went back into the dining room.

'He's something, isn't he?' Shelley whispered. She meant James but Jenna had eyes for only one man in the room. She gazed at Gus whose warm brown eyes were fixed on her with an intensity of desire and love.

'He absolutely is,' she agreed.